I0682035

Israeli Crossfire

Books by Stephen L. Thompson

The Crossfire Series

The SFO Series

Israeli Crossfire

Defending God's People

Stephen L. Thompson

Israeli Crossfire

The Crossfire team responds to a plea from the Israeli Mossad to help stop a possible terroristic threat by enemies who want to destroy all of the people in Israel.

The enemy of all mankind mounts an all-out campaign to derail or destroy the new Crossfire Team. The diabolical scheme increases in danger and threatens to engulf the entire world as the team races to save Israel only to find the terrorists have already accomplished their evil.

Now, as governments fail to stop the gruesome deaths of millions of men, women, and children, the Team turns to prayer because only God can now save the Israelis and other world targets.

- Stephen L. Thompson

Israeli Crossfire

Copyright © 2012 Stephen L. Thompson
All rights reserved. This book may not be duplicated or
reproduced in any form or manner whatsoever, except as
allowed by the U.S. Copyright Act of 1989, as amended,
without the prior and express written permission of the
publisher.

Published by
Stephen L. Thompson
Facebook.com/CrossfireNovelSeries

Unless otherwise noted, Scripture quotations are taken from
the HOLY BIBLE, NEW INTERNATIONAL VERSION®.
Copyright© 1973, 1978, 1984 by International Bible Society.
Used by permission of Zondervan Publishing House. All rights
reserved.

ISBN- 978-0-9850758-7-3

Published in the United States of America

Foreword

To my Christian readers –

The Crossfire series of action/adventure stories include depictions of violence which are unusual in Christian literature. It would be nice if there were no conflict or violence in our world. But we live in a time when evil is increasing instead of diminishing, when some men seem to be controlled by selfishness, madness, or evil forces. When the enemies of decent mankind are bent on subjugation of other men and women, righteous men and women must stand against evil. Please remember that the yoke of oppression is not lifted by prayer alone. God is our shepherd and we are his sheep. As long as there are wolves about, God will use some of us as sheep dogs to defend the rest of us. These stories are about people like that and the forces they fight against. The stories describe violence because it occurs in the real world and it is active in the lives of all people whether they recognize it or not.

To my non-Christian readers –

The Crossfire series include depictions of spiritual warfare and spiritual activity with which the non-Christian may not be familiar. These stories describe the realms and activities of both God and Satan because they are real and active in the lives of all people whether they recognize it or not.

Steve Thompson

NOTE: All characters, incidents, and venues described in this book are entirely the product of the author's imagination and remain the property of the author. This book and all text are the copyrighted property of the author and may not be copied or reproduced in any form without express written permission by the author.

CHAPTER ONE

The world had been a quiet place at midnight, with a full moon slowly sailing over the dark ground and giving a dim illumination to the trees, buildings, and people in sharp contrast to the glaringly bright lights of the active runways and terminal buildings in the background. A soft breeze swirled across the tarmac bringing a mixture of forgotten odors. To Sarah Cohen it now brought the sharp coppery smell of fresh blood mixed with the acrid tang of cordite.

The intense pain in her left leg burned with a sharp agony that demanded her immediate attention. "Too bad", the female Israeli Mossad agent thought, she didn't have time to attend to it right then. She used a mental technique she had been taught to reduce the autonomic response to the pain and pushed the pain away from her conscious mind. As a highly trained Mossad assassin she knew the danger of giving into the pain instead of continuing to fight on.

Sarah also was aware that the bullet that had slapped her leg out from under her was actually heaven sent because it had spun her around and knocked her to the ground. As she fell she felt, more than heard, several more rounds pass through the spot she had been standing in. Rolling over onto her stomach Sarah aimed her Uzi at their attackers who were back-lit by the hanger and taxiway lights.

The flashes of light from the dozen or so weapons firing at her made her think she could see the bullets coming directly at her. But her training and experience had shown her that it was just an illusion. She triggered a quick burst at one of the nearer attackers. To her disgust she saw him throw himself to the side and out of the way of her bullets.

As another round threw dirt into her face she reflected on the fact that it was at least good Israeli soil pelting her. "Oy, What a homecoming" she thought. She was intensely angry that she had been set up. Later she would remember that the

1

concept that she could be seriously maimed or killed never even crossed her mind. In her current life style this was just business as usual.

In a bid to rationalize why she was in this particularly bad situation her mind had one of those combat memory flashes which caused her to recall the last few minutes before they had touched down in her home country.

------------------------******------------------------

She remembered leaning back in the plush seat of the American CIA aircraft and gathering her thoughts as they approached the landing in Israel. The three-man American team she was guiding into Tel Aviv had so far refrained from grilling her on the details of the urgency of their newly assigned mission. But as they neared their destination she knew they would need input soon. She knew that with the sharp, inquisitive minds they had that her information had to be terse and accurate. It also had to provide sufficient detail to allow them to consider a wide range of possibilities.

Sarah found it hard to concentrate because in the last twenty-four hours she had rocketed across half the world in five hours, been shot at by tanks and ground-to-air missiles and just narrowly missed being obliterated in the middle of a nuclear explosion. Now by her own hand she had ushered herself and these new Christian friends of hers into another terribly dangerous situation without even time to sleep on it.

She remembered watching the moonlight on the Mediterranean Sea grow closer as the airplane descended into Ben Gurion Airport on the East Side of Tel Aviv. She mentally frowned as she realized that her two main problems were; first, that there were details that she wasn't allowed to tell anyone who wasn't in the Mossad, and second, there were other details she just did not know. No one knew and yet it was painfully critical to Israel that they find out those details very quickly.

It was almost midnight, local time, as they were vectored into the airport. Regardless of the unknowns, Sarah felt she could explain the situation well enough to get the team started. It wasn't a pretty picture.

Sarah looked over at Mark Connelly as he entered data into a laptop computer. She was fairly certain he was on the internet and updating his information concerning Israel and Tel Aviv and exploring any recent news on the area. She also knew he had sources that were not available to most people. Sources like the CIA, the NSA, and probably even her own agency. His quiet manner belied his strength and power. She had seen him in action. She coolly appraised his solid good looks and rugged features. She realized she was beginning to feel possessive about him and he wasn't even Jewish.

Mark stood about six foot, two inches and probably weighed in around 200 pounds. Dark brown-black hair framed a face that had 'honor' written all over it. His time in the United States Navy Seals had set his mold toward being a protector of the innocent. He thrived on complicated situations and was definitely an exceptional strategist of combat. The integrity he had in everything he did was like a giant rock foundation. He was a man you could count on to keep his word even if he had to die for it. Oh, he had his faults, but then who didn't? He was a very detailed planner, but then if the situation went into the unknown he was just as quick to throw the plans out the window and go on instinct and training.

Mark's physique was what the average American thought of when they pictured the perfect Marine. An honor scout personality in a body like that of Arnold Schwarzenegger. He was bulked out somewhat but, as she had seen, when he worked out it was more for greater endurance than physical bulk. Whatever, it made him a man who could turn a girl's head just by walking by. That bothered her somehow. Hmm.

Sarah glanced back at Jack and Laura Malone sitting together in the back seats. These two people were also something else. Their Christian faith was so absolute and matter of fact that one never doubted that each one had an ongoing personal relationship with their Jesus. Yet they didn't act superior or even smug about their theology. If anything, they had become more humble since she had met them.

Jack was a good-looking young man with blond hair and gray-green eyes. He normally dominated any scene he was a part of. It was what was called a "command presence." He stood about six foot four inches and was, in his own way, just as muscularly solid as Mark was. His muscle mass was more fluid and compact and he didn't show the 'buffed' shape that Mark did. But he was anything but soft. He was a good fighter and didn't ask any quarter in a conflict. She ought to know. He had beaten her at unarmed combat in the field and that was something nobody else had done since her early Mossad training days.

Jack's wife, Laura, was a beautiful and refined young woman with a full head of blonde hair and light green eyes. Certainly the most amateur at combat of the team, she had a sharp mind and a grit and determination that sustained and complimented Jack's physical attributes. There was a synergism between her devotion and her husband's growing combat capabilities. Sarah's Judaism had been sorely tried as she had watched the young couple's faith effectively demonstrated in the past few days. Certain recent events could not be dismissed as coincidences because it was definitely God working through their lives. They prayed, God listened and things happened! God spoke to them and they obeyed without question or hesitation. She could feel in her deepest soul that what they were doing was inherently right. When she was with them at stressful times she could actually sense God's presence and involvement. This disturbed her deeply because it ran against her upbringing and her early religious training.

Sarah considered herself introspectively. Her mandatory military training had led to her recruitment by the premier intelligence service of her country, the Mossad. Her training and operational background had hardened her attitude but, so far, not her looks. She knew she was a darker-haired version of Laura with a decidedly darker background. She also knew she weighed about 150 pounds and stood right at five foot ten inches tall. She frowned to herself, "Only three months in America and I'm already thinking in their terms. I'm really 68 kilograms and 178 centimeters!"

Her thoughts were interrupted by the whine of the landing gear and the 'thump' as they locked into landing position. The plane began to vibrate due to the wind drag on the lowered gear and the engines sped up slightly to overcome the new resistance. Lining up on the main runway at Ben Gurion the heavily modified business jet landed with almost no bounce and quickly slowed. Sarah was impressed with the technology of the United States and the capabilities of the military pilot. But, she was glad to be coming home. Time in the Gentile world had been isolation from the home world and familiar food and rituals she was used to.

As the plane pulled off the runway onto a taxiway, the tower directed them to a private hanger away from the main terminal. Sarah unbuckled her seat belt and walked up to the cockpit. Something wasn't right. Her contact had not mentioned meeting them at a special hanger. It would be stupid because the action could pinpoint them to anyone watching.

Sarah's heightened instincts caused her to sharply focus on the people standing just inside the hanger they were heading toward. Immediately she noted that there was no one from her agency there. Worse than that she saw two men she knew to be local crime scene 'muscle'. Quickly walking back into the passenger cabin her worried expression was rewarded with immediate attention from the other three people. She pointed out the window, "Those aren't my people, and we've got trouble." Mark picked up the intercom phone and urgently talked to Major Mike White, the pilot. Sarah pulled a digital cell phone out of her bag and speed-dialed her contact. Jack reached under the seat and pulled out a bag with weapons in it and started taking them out.

Feeling the sudden tension and danger, Laura started praying quietly, "Jesus, cover each one here with your blood and put your angels around them. Warrior angels to protect us Lord and it is in your name I pray all these things Jesus, watch over us."

The plane suddenly braked to a halt just outside the open hanger. The aircraft landing lights that had been shut off flared out and starkly illuminated the people inside the hanger. Most of the people turned away from the lights or put their hand in front of their eyes. Except one man who started to draw a weapon from under his jacket. The plane's engines quickly ran up in retro power and the plane made a startlingly quick retreat from the hanger. Sarah nodded to herself. She had been right about the U. S. Air Force pilot. He was good. Using the ground steering and engine thrust he swung the plane around to its left while still moving backward. As the plane came about the pilot disengaged the engine retro braking and the engine thrust increased suddenly. The exhaust blast knocked down several of the people who had run out of the hanger with drawn weapons. The plane quickly pulled away from the hanger and back onto the taxiway toward the main terminal.

Sarah was standing in the aisle carrying on a rapid conversation in Hebrew on her phone when the plane suddenly jerked to a halt again. Grabbing onto a seat back to keep from falling, she looked out the cockpit windshield. She saw a fuel truck had pulled across the taxi strip. The plane was effectively blocked to the front and she was sure that there would be no escape to the rear this time either. She spoke one command on the phone and let it drop to the seat next to her. She bent over and retrieved the 9mm Uzi machine gun from her carryall and racked a round into the chamber then headed to the side door of the aircraft.

Even though they couldn't see behind them, the team didn't panic concerning the apparent trap. They just began to react in a trained way to deal with the situation. Jack checked that the magazine in his hand was full and snapped it into the

.223 caliber Colt CAR-15. He then racked the slide back and chambered a live round in the rifle. Putting it on safety he loaded a second one for Mark and a third one for Laura. Handing out a handful of extra magazines from the weapons bag to each person, he then moved to the door in front of his wife.

The team was ready to fight as the door raised and lowered into position. Even though it was dark outside the door, Sarah didn't hesitate. She saw that the grass at the edge of the taxiway was only two feet from the side of the plane. She went down two steps and threw herself away from the aircraft in a well-executed tuck and roll. Following her example, Jack, Laura, and Mark were right behind her in exiting the doorway.

The snap and whine of bullets slamming through the air and hitting the aircraft body behind them was intimidating, but each of the team knew that the only way to live through this was to fight back hard rather than huddle on the ground. Sarah turned toward the fuel truck in time to catch the man in an expensive suit firing a handgun at arm's length, running toward them from the open door of the vehicle. Snapping the Uzi up Sarah sent a quick five-round burst at the man. She watched his feet fly out in front of him as the bullets slammed his body backward in a bloody spray. Professional field agent that she was she still trembled slightly when she realized the burst of bullets took out the gunman without hitting the fuel truck!

Mark saw a small car headed toward them from the hanger area. The bright winking lights on his side of the vehicle indicated shooters that wanted to give the team a permanent place in Israel, underground! He sighted his rifle and fired a three-round burst at the windshield in front of the driver. Unfortunately for the driver, the hurriedly selected vehicle had no armor-plating or bulletproof glass. The first two rounds starred the windshield but ricocheted off into the air. But the third round went through the damaged glass and struck the driver in the forehead. Traveling at roughly four thousand feet per second, the fifty-five grain boat tail slug snapped the driver's head back. The two men in the back seat didn't have time to notice because the car, steered by the now-dead driver, swerved abruptly to the left and flipped into the air. Coming down hard onto the concrete the top crumpled into the interior, crushing the life out of the two remaining attackers.

There were still about twelve people running toward them from the hanger and firing a variety of weapons. The team was fortunate that running and shooting at the same time doesn't work very well. But, it still seemed like an army trying to kill them. Small chunks of ground were blown into the air and bullets seemed to be everywhere. A bullet hit Jack's right shoe and took a chunk of leather and part of the heel off the shoe. Another round took some of Laura's hair with it and made a lot more of it stand-up when she realized how close that bullet had been. In response, Jack and Laura both started firing their rifles toward the runners. They were rewarded with one person stumbling and falling to the ground. But the numbers were too great. There were still too many guns shooting at them and getting too close too quickly.

Sarah was firing short bursts from the Uzi but with a three-inch barrel the accuracy at this range was limited. A bullet slammed into her left leg and knocked her down, as much from the surprise as from imparted energy.

-----------------------******-----------------------

The memory rushed back into focus, with the present for Sarah.

Laura was sighting on one runner when a sudden explosion and loud shrieking noise jarred her from behind. She whipped her head around and saw an awesome sight. Mike White had joined the fight and he looked like something out of a Sylvester Stallone movie. He held a minigun with both hands and at his feet was a large ammo can with a belt of bullets running up to the minigun. The eight barrels were spinning rapidly, pumping out over three thousand rounds per minute. The flame from the front of the gun was a continual flare about two feet in length. Laura looked back at their attackers and watched as the minigun chopped them down like a chainsaw.

The last man standing flew backward and the minigun stopped firing. The decreasing whine of the minigun's motor was the only noise she could hear. Silence settled on that part of the airfield. Jack and Mark got to their feet and moving cautiously with their CAR-15s held ready, started toward the enemy to see if there was anyone left alive.

As the huge cloud of gun smoke from the minigun wafted past her, Laura glanced over at Sarah and saw her huddled on the ground. A flash of fear shot through Laura. She dropped her rifle and ran over to where Sarah was laying on the ground holding her leg. She had blood on her pants and hands and a major scowl on her face. Seeing Laura approach, she managed a weak smile and said, "Welcome to Israel."

Laura moved Sarah's hands and examined the bloody wound on her leg. At least it wasn't pulsing blood, so no major arteries had been hit. Laura reached over and pulled out Sarah's combat knife. Then Laura cut the left sleeve of her shirt and pulled it off. She made two pads out of the material and pressed them tightly against the entrance and exit wounds to staunch the flow of blood.

She had Sarah hold the pads as she cut off her other sleeve and bound the pads to the wounds by tying it around Sarah's leg. She then helped her to her feet. Sarah may have been wounded and in pain, but she hung onto her Uzi and kept a sharp watch all around. Her training and experience as a field combatant had been thorough.

CHAPTER TWO

As the adrenaline slowly left his system, Jack realized that the whole action had taken less than five minutes. The very efficient IDF, the Israeli Defense Force, and the local police were just starting to arrive.

Checking the bodies of their attackers, neither of the men could find any signs of life. Jack quietly asked God to forgive them for having taken the lives of the men and women they had shot. He didn't feel bad about shooting them in self-defense, he just wasn't sure it had been God's will and he honestly admitted he hadn't taken the time to ask the Lord first before he started shooting. The approaching sirens and other noises faded into the background as Jack felt the nearness of the Lord. While he didn't sense any approval, he also did not sense any reproach. He had learned that the Lord will honor the efforts of those that love Him and try to follow Him even when they act hastily. He thanked the Lord that they had survived the attack and especially that Laura hadn't been injured or killed.

Just then Sarah limped up to them with Laura supporting her left side. Laura's improvised bandage seemed to have stanched the flow of blood from the wound in Sarah's leg. The whole left leg of Sarah's jeans was soaked in her blood and she was definitely paler than normal.

The Major had put his mini-gun back into the aircraft storage area and came over with a flashlight. As a variety of vehicles came to a halt near them, the group went from one attacker to the next looking at their faces with the flashlight. Sarah shook her head. "I can only positively identify two. They are low level enforcers in the Tel Aviv crime scene. I don't know any of the others."

By then dozens of people crowded up to them and the scene was dissolving into chaos with everyone talking at once, some in Hebrew and some in English.

An English command rang out for them to drop their weapons. There was no compromise with the order. The team lowered their weapons to the ground and stood away from them. Sarah let Laura put hers down for her. Armed members of the IDF approached them with their weapons up and aimed at the team amid the strobe lights glaring from five or six different emergency vehicles.

Another voice amplified by an electronic bullhorn rang out and effectively stilled everyone. The commands were in Hebrew but had a decidedly authoritarian ring. Everyone but the team backed up and moved away, fifteen or twenty feet.

Mark looked at Sarah with a raised eyebrow. She nodded, "Yes, those are my people. They are asking everyone else to stay out of a Central Institute crime scene for the moment." She looked around at the people near them. "These people are smart. They do not want to get us mad at them for disobeying a request like this."

Mark looked beyond the circle of people surrounding them and saw a great number of Israeli military personnel establishing a perimeter around an area that included their aircraft. The shootout at Ben Gurion was getting a major reaction. Mark realized that one reason could be that the security forces were caught flat-footed and this battle could well be a major embarrassment from their viewpoint.

Several men and a woman with identification badges had come from the area of the bullhorn and firmly, but respectively, herded the team and the pilot away from the center of attention and into the relative darkness and calm next to a large SUV. Some others checked and photographed each of the dead men and collected the weapons. One of them collected the weapons the team had laid on the ground.

Another agent spoke to the pilot. He nodded and approached the team. Smiling he shook hands all around. "Look, I can't tell you how much I really enjoyed our time together. Nice flight, good gunfight. Yeah, one thing that lets me sleep like a baby is a midnight gunfight after a little bit of World War Three." The cynical comments were relieved by

Mike's smile. "These folks are in touch with my folks and I'm going to take care of the plane for now. I'll be here for the next few hours..." He stopped and looked at the newly repaired aircraft that had absorbed some new damage from the ground fire. "Okay, maybe the next few days. If you need a ride again, just call the USAF and ask for me, okay?"

Mark smiled and shook the pilot's hand, "Next time, Mike." Jack also shook his hand and said, "Mike thanks for everything. If you need some top level support, we can make a phone call."

Mike smiled and shook his head, "I've got this. It's already taken care of, thanks."

Jack tipped his head and smiled at the pilot. "Take care and go with God." Sarah smiled at him and waved from her position against the SUV. She wasn't up to big good-byes right then. Laura gave him a hug, thanked him for his ride earlier in the Lightening II, and promised that they would be in touch. He grinned at the team, turned and walked off with the agent. The Major had no clue to how quickly he would be reminded of his offer to fly this group again.

A slim man in his thirties stepped forward and took Sarah's hand. He was dressed in a stylish white turtleneck sweater under an expensive suit. She waved the rest of the team over and introduced him. His name was David Zahavy and he was Sarah's direct supervisor and control agent. The two of them were obviously on good terms with a casual and unspoken ease in their relationship that spoke of a history of shared dangers.

David spoke excellent English with a slight East Coast accent. He looked at the team and shook his head. "This is not the welcome I had prepared for your introduction to Israel. My agency and I personally, ask your forgiveness at allowing these vermin to attack you as they did. We are embarrassed by this lapse in security. It was only your bravery and professional ability that made up for our slip and we will remember that."

David's air of professionalism and class were clearly evident. So was the fact that as a supervisor he had an empathy with his agents. His graceful, precise motions reassured those around him that he was in control and they could count on his ability. His dress and mannerisms were what the British call impeccable.

His face lit up somewhat as he looked at Mark. He reached out and shook Mark's hand. "Mr. Connelly, I've wanted to meet you for some time. I have followed your career and exploits for several years now. Ever since you and your team of SEALs helped prevent a terrible massacre on the Israeli cruise ship of the Zim Line while they were in American waters. I understood at the time that you had 'bent' your orders and put yourself and your team in harm's way to protect Israeli citizens. In this country we honor those who defend us." He smiled, which seemed to come naturally to his face.

"The fact is that you made the raid a success despite the odds against you. Your officers could not publicly honor that operation but we covertly added our appreciation to your record and they agreed. But let me tell you that your ingenious scheme is still talked about in intelligence circles in Israel. Personally, I greatly respect your integrity and professionalism." David waved his hand to include the whole team. "That goes for all of you. I hope our operation here together will have the same success that you have achieved in your other assignments."

At that point Sarah's left leg had taken all the abuse it wanted; so it quit working. She felt faint and started to fall. Seeing her predicament, Laura grabbed her by the arm and held her up. She maneuvered Sarah over to the open back doors of the SUV and made her sit down. David snapped his fingers and pointed at Sarah's leg. One of the agents left at a run and came back quickly with a medical attendant. The attendant removed the makeshift bandage, cut away her pants leg, and proceeded to check the wound. Looking up at David he spoke rapid Hebrew. David nodded and the attendant spoke into his radio. A minute later an ambulance pulled up and two men pulled an EMS gurney from the back. They put Sarah on the gurney and put her into the ambulance. She was accompanied by two other Mossad agents.

David watched her go and turned back to the three other team members. "She will be all right. The medic felt her wound should be tended to under better conditions. They'll take her to Tel Hashomer Hospital so that it can be handled properly."

Mark smiled, "I'd guess those other two agents of yours will be with her until she returns, right?" David nodded. Mark's eyes narrowed as he watched the ambulance leave. "Good" he said quietly. One of David's eyebrows rose slightly and he looked from Mark toward his disappearing agent.

Having ascertained that none of the others were injured, he asked them to join him in the SUV. Two of the Mossad agents brought their collected weapons and their hand luggage from the CIA jet and placed everything in the back of the SUV.

The SUV was smooth and comfortable as they drove through the city. Jack looked at David and made a comment. "I notice that no one seemed very upset by the action tonight. Concerned, but not unduly affected. Does this kind of thing go on all the time here?"

David looked at Jack in the mirror. "You both need to understand something very basic about this country, Mr. and Mrs. Malone." He was deadly serious. "We do not live at peace like the majority of your country does. Every willing and able-bodied citizen here has spent time in the military and is always aware that the hatred by violent groups that surround Israel can turn deadly in an instant. Anywhere, anytime, suicide bombers, car bombings, rocket attacks, random shooting and other forms of quick death are our constant companions. No one ever feels completely at ease." He thought for a second. "No one with any sense, that is. We tend to operate more on a casual survival basis than a freedom basis. Every intelligent Israeli is serious about the national defense and their individual protection. It's not what we would like, but it's what we have to do to live." He seemed angry that it had to be that way.

Mark was nodding his head and added, "It's like living in the rear areas of a combat zone. While you're not on the front lines you are still at war with the enemy and he will strike you when and where he can. You can't really let down your guard for a moment because that will be the weakness the enemy is waiting for."

David agreed with Mark's diagnosis. "I spent five years in the United States and I envy your people their life style. I don't think most of them realize how good they have it, and many abuse their privileges, but I still envy the peace they have."

Mark turned and smiled at Jack and Laura in the Captain's seats behind him. "Just think like you are spies in enemy territory and one slip will kill us all. Okay?"

Jack and Laura both nodded. Laura smiled a lopsided smile at her husband, "I guess we aren't on a vacation." They all laughed at that.

Mark glanced at David as he drove. He knew some things about Sarah's boss although he hadn't mentioned it before. He knew that David had sought out the Mossad while he was doing his obligatory military duty. The man had been intent on becoming the best that the organization had. His dedication and intelligence had led quickly to premier assignments and promotions. He had rough times and made mistakes, but comparatively speaking, he was worth twice as much as other agents to a supervisor when he was on an assignment in those days.

Mark knew that David never risked anything if he could plan it so that there was little or no risk. He wouldn't assign an agent to a job he himself couldn't do. Of course there was little that he couldn't do, so the bar was set fairly high. According to a file Mark had read, David's personal motto was to see a job through to the end and he never, ever left an agent out in the cold.

Mark also knew that David knew his limitations and abilities. He had refused his latest offered promotion because it would take him out of the field and strictly into politics. His primary interest seemed to be with the field craft of his people.

As he steered the SUV through Tel Aviv's deserted streets, David was acutely aware of Mark's study of him. But, Laura's vacation comment sent David's thoughts back to another "peaceful urban combat zone" event in his early days as a Mossad agent.

-------------------------*＊＊＊＊＊*-------------------------

He had been directed to make a deal in Paris, with two Europeans from one of the, then splintering, Russian satellite countries. They were brokering a multi-million dollar deal for two Russian nuclear warheads. David had managed to pare the potential buyers down to three by raising the amount he was willing to offer for the weapons. This was the final meeting to determine who the buyer would be and make arrangements for a swap of the warheads for the cash. Since his control agent supervisor had instructed him to raise his bid to ten million dollars U.S. he felt he could outbid the competition and make the deal. Then, when the sellers produced the weapons they would have them arrested by the French police and the nuclear weapons could be taken off the market.

It would not be a long meeting. David was sure of that. In the early nineties not many of the terrorist organizations had ten million dollars to spend.

He met the sellers for the third time on the fourth floor of the business building at eight o'clock at night. Everyone else had gone home and they were alone. Two other Mossad agents were on the streets outside as backup.

The bid was easily the high bid and everything was going well when a third member of the selling team joined them. David knew this Algerian very well. The problem was that he also knew David. For a shocked second the new man didn't know what to do. Then he made up his mind to expose David's undercover role to the two sellers and their bodyguards.

Thinking quickly David stood up and pointed at the Algerian and yelled, "I know him! He's with the Surete (the French police)!" Pulling out his pistol from his belt David fired one shot into the Algerian's head killing him instantly.

The bodyguards had their guns out now but were unsure what to do. David pointed his pistol at the sellers and accused them of being part of a French trap to catch him. He quickly backed out of the nearest door and shut it.

He knew that after a few seconds consideration the sellers would figure out what the real deal was and then they would be after him in a flash. They couldn't let him live with what he knew.

David ran by the elevators and reached in and punched the ground floor button on the first one. He then ran to the stairs to throw off any pursuit. As part of the door frame to the stairwell exploded into fragments he realized that they were reacting quicker than he had hoped. Now he wished he'd taken the elevator.

Rushing fleetly up the stairs he exited the stairwell two flights above the fourth floor and hurried across the darkened hall to an office that was closed and locked. He heard the shoes pounding on the stairs behind him.

He didn't know if they were coming up or going down but he ignored them as he jimmied the lock. The door swung open and he stepped into the dark office. Quietly shutting the door he heard it lock again. Staying low and away from the windows so as to not throw a shadow against the frosted glass of the door, he hurried over to the window and looked out.

He was six floors above the ground and knew he had four men looking for him. He rethought that and decided it could be more because he wasn't sure where the Algerian had come from and that could mean additional troops for the sellers.

David had military training and experience and he knew his tradecraft from top to bottom. He decided to throw some smoke their way and then go on the offensive. The best defense is a good offense.

Carefully opening the window he looked around the office. Taking the knife from his pocket he cut off a thirty-foot section of phone line from one of the desks. Tying a stapler onto the end of the line he went out onto the fire-escape and lowered the stapler until it was even with the window in the end of the hall on the fourth floor. Making three big swings of the pendulum he smashed the stapler through the window and brought it back out. Hoisting it quickly he jumped back into the office and peered out the window looking down at the scene of his destruction.

When he saw a head poked out, he retreated and went back to the door. Carefully unlocking it and checking the hall he couldn't sense anyone on that floor. Screwing a short but effective silencer onto the end of his weapon, he checked the action for proper operation. Slipping out of the office and back to the stairwell he heard two people coming down from the roof exit. They were coming quickly but not with any urgency. So they hadn't seen him on the fire escape from the roof.

He waited until they passed his floor and then opened the door quietly and with two silenced shots he ended both of their careers. Their bodies tumbled together down to the next landing. David calmly walked back to the elevator and took it back to the fourth floor. As he expected, the other two men had run to the stairwell to see what happened to their men.

Checking his backtrack he walked up silently behind the two sellers who were looking at the bodies of their bodyguards with dismay. It was easy to capture and disarm them both and not having any handcuffs, he made them lay on the floor and used their belts to tie their hands together and to their feet. That way they couldn't move.

Checking the office where the deal had been in progress he only found the body of the Algerian. Going out to the broken window at the end of the hall he was amazed how big a mess the stapler had made.

David leaned out the broken window and called to his backup in Hebrew. Rewarded with an answer he watched a few minutes later as a large truck backed up to the freight dock of the building and the two Europeans were 'crated' for shipment to Israel.

David left the mess for the office janitors to find the next morning and accompanied his men and their captives back to their country. The only difference was that the three of them rode in the passenger compartment of the El Al aircraft.

It took less than a day to learn where the stolen nuclear warheads were and a local team made sure the French authorities found them. Because the European sellers had openly advocated the use of the weapons against the tiny nation of Israel they were given permanent residency in the best Israeli prison.

-------------------------******-----------------------

David checked his mirror and thought about how the people in the back of the SUV had probably never had to deal with people hunting them down to kill them. "Ah! But then again, who knew?"

CHAPTER THREE

David drove quickly through the more or less deserted streets of Tel Aviv in the early morning hours. He turned into a building on a main street. Pressing a device that looked like a garage door opener he was rewarded with a door opening in the covered front part of the building. Seeing Mark's quizzical look he handed the "opener" to him as he drove into the building.

Mark examined the device and handed it back with a smile. "Nice little arrangement, that."

David looked at him with additional respect as he finished parking. "You didn't look at it very long. I would be interested in knowing what you were able to determine."

Mark got out of the vehicle in the underground parking area. There was solid concrete with lots of echoes and strange noises coming from everywhere. He walked around the SUV and met David as Jack and Laura disembarked from the back door on the driver's side.

Mark waved his hand at the now-closed garage door. "My guess is that device merely notifies your building security team that you want access to the garage area. Somehow, they were able to scan our vehicle and determine that it would be all right for us to enter. The reason I like it is because it is like honking your horn. You don't have any control except to announce yourself and present yourself for scrutiny. The security team can admit you, deny you, or burn you as they need to. That about sum it up?"

David laughed, "Yes, mostly, except that the Motorola cameras that were activated by the device allowed the computers to do a digital comparison of each of our faces before the door opened. The vehicle itself provided our body mass specification telemetry. In less time than it takes to tell it, the system authenticated each of us and gave security a green light to let us in. While we were sitting out there the vehicle was also electronically inspected for unknown and mysterious additions inside or outside to prevent car bombs from getting into the garage.

As they walked to the elevator Laura remembered the Oklahoma City bombing of the Federal building and agreed that it paid to be careful. "It would be very easy to bring this building down with a car bomb in this garage."

As the doors closed on the elevator David agreed, "Even with the sophisticated security and precautions we don't take chances. He pushed the 11th floor button and the elevator started off. But it did some very strange things. First, it went down several floors, not up. Then it stopped descending and started moving forward! It built up a considerable amount of speed before slowing to a stop again. Then it began to go down again. Finally it stopped and the doors opened into an efficient office space.

Laura looked at David, "Did this elevator car do what I think it just did?"

He nodded to her question. "We are eleven stories underground and four blocks from the garage. That 'building' above the garage is only a façade. There are no people anywhere near there." He smiled at the look of intelligence on her face. "War zone thinking, remember?"

She nodded, "I like it."

They walked into a spacious conference room with a large table in the middle of the room and ten chairs ranged around it. The room had light wood paneling and indirect lighting. Light green carpeting muted the 'office' tone while the entire ceiling was aglow with a light that looked like the early morning sky beyond a window.

Everyone grabbed a chair and after inquiring of their desires for food and drink, David called somewhere and within a few minutes a tray of fruits and sweetbreads was brought into the conference room along with a variety of soft drinks and water. David pushed a button on the conference table and a section of the table in front of each person slid back to expose a computer monitor and other conference equipment.

He picked up a headset with a miniature Star-set like microphone and ear piece and put it on. His voice then came out of the speakers at each position.

"Let's go over what happened when you landed, one by one. After everyone has finished we'll do a brainstorm session. The microphone in front of you will do the recording, so just speak in a normal manner."

Mark reported everything in sequence as he remembered it, followed by Laura and then Jack. After they had finished the debriefing, Mark kicked off the idea session with a pointed question to David. "Who were those people and how did they know we were coming?"

David sat back and considered. These Americans were here to help his people. They had already put their lives on the line for his country in Libya and right here in Israel. They deserved every bit of information he was allowed to give them. And maybe some he wasn't allowed to give them.

"First, let me be perfectly honest with you. I don't know, yet, how they knew you were coming and when you would arrive. But as to who they are I have a better understanding." He stopped and took a drink of water while he arranged his mental notes.

"Who were the people who attacked you? Hired thugs working for a shadow organization based in Tel Aviv but directly controlled by the Arab Strike Force or ASF, working out of Palestine, Libya, and Iran. These people, as I'm sure you know, want to exterminate everyone in Israel and every other Jew in the world also."

"Our informants have only been able to give us a sketchy picture of what this organization is doing here in Israel. More threads of information or hints, woven together into a loose tapestry of hate and death."

David looked grim as he continued. "We know that there is a plan in the works that will damage, if not destroy, the State of Israel in the next three weeks if we cannot stop it. But that is almost all we know."

Mark asked, "Why do you need us?"

David stood up and paced behind the chairs. "Because we believe that the main group of conspirators is located at an American business concern which, apparently, has a security system similar to our own. We have tried a variety of personnel, but not one has been able to enter the business. They are stopped at the desk and refused admission. This is not illegal. They have the right to allow in whomever they feel should be in there and keep out whomever they want to. We have made 'Official' inspections of the business but have found nothing because they knew we were coming and were prepared. Nighttime sorties have been, shall we say, less than successful. The touchy part of this is that the majority of the business is legitimate, successful, and very important to Israel as an asset as well as to Israeli-American relations."

David stopped pacing and looked at Jack and Laura. "We had hoped to introduce you two as American business executives looking into the software being developed here with an eye toward a major purchase. We felt that you would have an opportunity to get into the building and be shown almost everything in an effort to win your business." He shook his head, "The reception you got at the airport took away your 'innocent' status and probably derailed your effectiveness."

Mark had been following this from his own viewpoint. "Why would that change anything? None of the opposition at the airport had a chance to identify any of us and if they did, they took it to the grave with them." Mark let his eyes drift up to the ceiling. "Of course, this is true only if your people prevented anyone else who was there from getting away."

"Good point. We think we had the place sewed up very quickly. But we don't know that for truth and I for one don't want to endanger you people if the operational cover has already been blown." David was obviously willing to be persuaded to keep going and that is what Mark did.

"All right, let's just test your theory. We will have Jack and Laura as the executives and I can be their bodyguard." Mark was planning again.

Jack scratched one of his sideburns and asked, "If they have access to your files, then we will be known already."

David shook his head, "They don't have access to our files. But they may have files on recently retired American military personnel." He looked pointedly at Mark with a slight lift to his eyebrows, daring Mark to prove him wrong. He couldn't.

Laura piped up. "Okay, let us say we do this. What are we going to wear? It wouldn't look right for two high level executives to show up in jeans and pullovers or full combat gear and that is all we have with us."

David nodded. "Yes, we will have to go shopping soon. First, I suggest we have breakfast."

The team traveled through several office complexes and through a large atrium with a lot of plants and people relaxing from the underground environment in the park like setting. Jack noticed a few veiled looks of distrust, dislike, or even borderline hatred on an occasional face as they passed. He was sure their status as important Americans was the cause for these attitudes. It could also be their avowed Christianity. While the Jewish people and Christians shared the Old Testament, the New Testament was disliked, dismissed, or not even thought about by the majority of Israelis.

Jack was aware that in this country, Jesus was known by the name of Yahshua and was seen by many either as an extremist false messiah or a good but martyred Jewish rabbi (teacher). Roughly twenty percent of the Hebrew population has no interest in religion. Most religious Jews do not consider Yahshua at all, except for the Messianic Jews and Hebrew Christians (which are a small fraction of the population), Jews do not believe he was the Messiah, Son of God, or that he rose from the dead. Lately, some of the most scholarly teachers that researched the New Testament and verified the hundreds of prophesies that Yahshua had fulfilled, had come to agree that he was a Messiah and that He had risen from the dead. But they still saw Him as a Messiah only for the Gentiles. They felt the Jewish Messiah was yet to come. Still, many Jews do not appreciate Americans because of the influence that the United States has as the major supporter of the beleaguered nation.

A cafeteria style restaurant was serving breakfast and had some American egg and meat dishes. On David's advice they stayed away from beef and settled on cheese omelets and rolls. There was a large variety of fruit and sweetbreads available, also. David was recognized as he entered and the group was shown to a private dining room where they ordered their food.

As they were waiting, a commotion occurred outside the doors to the room. David listened to his headset for a few seconds and rose to go to the doors when they were forcibly opened and a waiter stumbled into the room and fell down. He got up yelling in Hebrew when Sarah limped into the room on crutches and stared at him.

He turned an angry face to David who soothed things over and walked the waiter to the door and then shut it behind him. By then Sarah had limped over to the table and let herself down into one of the chairs being very careful of her left leg. When David returned with a frown she spoke in English. "My leg hurts to stand on it. That, that," … she mentally fumbled for the correct phrase in any language, "Person, told me that this was a private party and I could not come in here! I just convinced him that he was wrong." Her expression dared David to give her any grief about it.

Knowing Sarah as he did, David took the high road and avoided discipline or arguments. "Next time use your communicator. We would have come and brought you in ourselves."

Chastised, but not broken, Sarah turned to the table and looking at the team asked what she had missed.

Laura figured Sarah knew about the elevator so she told her about the discussion they were having and asked how things went at the hospital. Sarah made a small face. "They irrigated the wound for about an hour to reduce any additional scarring or infection. The bullet grazed my leg halfway between my knee and my backside and gave me a gash that is about three inches long and a couple of millimeters deep. The doctor had to use sutures because I lost the outer layer of skin over the gash. He said I will have a major scar but that nothing important like major arteries or bone was struck. The hardest part was watching them pull little tiny pieces of 'Monarchy" jeans out of the wound with tweezers!"

Jack asked how much pain she was in and if they had given her anything to counter it. She shook her head, "The only thing we can take is Aspirin. Anything heavier could cloud my judgment or make me talk when I shouldn't. The pain is now like a major ache and I can tolerate it. I will be off these crutches by this afternoon. I just need to let the trauma settle down before I start using it fully."

After breakfast everyone agreed that jet lag was dragging at them and they needed some rest. There were guest rooms in the complex and it wasn't very long until everyone but David was sound asleep. They would seek out some better clothes that afternoon.

CHAPTER FOUR

That afternoon, the group left the garage and traveled down Dizengoff to a strip mall at Dizengoff Square, a block south of the Cameri Theater. Another car with three agents in it accompanied them on their shopping trip as security for the team. Sarah had a definite limp but was determined not to let her injury keep her from shopping. The day was pleasant without too much heat this late in the afternoon.

After managing to find several changes of clothing, the team felt better. Jack and Laura were able to find suitable 'executive' attire. Jack, Laura, and Mark had not had anything to change into since they flew out of the airbase in Italy while chasing a terrorist named Max Lister.

The strip mall was a bright and hustling place with people coming in and going out of the stores everywhere. Some were strollers just window shopping while others were more focused and were coming and going somewhere definite. Some people sat or stood outside the stores and just watched the throngs moving along the sidewalk. One of these was a small man with casual clothing. He was dark Caucasian with close-set eyes. Those eyes grew larger when he saw the group moving toward him with David in their midst. His orders were specific. "Kill the woman." But which woman?" he thought. There were two of them. "Oh Well" he thought, "I will just kill them both!" His hand slid carefully under his shirt and touched the handgun hidden there. Just a few steps closer, closer, NOW!

Laura had joined Sarah at the front of the group to ask about acceptable fashion trends in Israel when David suddenly jumped between them and knocked them to the sidewalk. Just then two shots rang out and David fell backward in a shower of blood.

One of the security agents fired a short burst of 9MM rounds from an Uzi machine pistol into the small man who had just shot David. The man dropped his pistol and tried to stem his life's blood leaking out of his chest. He looked confused as he slowly collapsed where he stood.

Mark took a defensive position between the dead man and where David had fallen, in case there were other attackers. In surprisingly little time the strip mall was almost deserted. When the shots rang out, most people fell to the ground or sought cover in a nearby store. As soon as the shooting stopped, they made themselves scarce. Other than the security detail and the team, there wasn't a soul within two hundred feet.

Sarah crawled over to David. He did not look good. His color had paled already and one of the bullets had hit a lung because he had a sucking chest wound. The other round had taken him a bit lower, somewhere below his heart. His breathing was rapid and shallow and he tried to talk but couldn't. Sarah cradled his head in her lap and felt hot tears welling up in her eyes as she straightened his hair.

Jack had helped Laura up and she stood there with her hand over her mouth looking in shock at David's form on the ground. She started to pray for him. "Dear Jesus, this man saved my life, please help him." This was a very heartfelt prayer. She was about to continue when Sarah looked up from the floor and held out one bloodied hand. Looking directly at Laura she said only one word, but you could tell it came from the bottom of her soul. "Please"

Jack saw his wife close her eyes and start to say something. But she stopped in mid-breath and quietly said, "Oh, Oh, my God!" Her eyes flew open and there was a look on her face that Jack had never seen before. It was almost imperious, very authoritarian and one that would not accept defiance.

Laura pointed and told him to kneel on the other side of David's limp form. She knelt on the side closest to where she was standing. When she looked at Jack he still didn't recognize whoever it was looking back at him. She said, "Place your hands on him and pray to almighty Yahveh that he will be healed." Jack didn't recognize her voice either. Normally, a pleasant contralto, Laura's voice had gotten more forceful and seemed to have an echo. Sort of like a strong soprano with an alto echo which seemed a fraction of a second behind. It reminded him of two people trying to read the same words at the same time. As he placed his hands on David's chest, Jack realized that David had died because he had ceased to breathe.

Laura turned her head and looked directly into Sarah's eyes. Sarah was shocked to her very soul. This Christian friend of hers had become so commanding that Sarah felt awe. Laura told her, "Do not doubt! Do not let religious differences hinder you. Pray with your heart, not your head." Laura placed her hands on David's chest. Things had grown strangely quiet and Jack felt like the little tableau he was part of was isolated from the world right then. He prayed with the sincerity of heart to a God he knew was hearing him.

Looking upward, Laura started to speak. "Heavenly Father Yahveh, you are awesome beyond words. Angels and men bow before you in reverent fear and love. Yahshua, when you walked on this earth you prayed to the Father to heal many Jews as a sign of the Father's power and compassion. Father, as you were yesterday, you are today and will be forever. Yahveh, heal David, son of Hiram of the house of Benjamin for your glory and to show the world your love."

Jack felt the power of the Lord bear strongly down on him and his arms and hands got hot. It seemed like all creation vibrated around him.

Sarah's religious training had never included how to understand or handle the direct touch of God. Her heart felt like it would explode in her chest. Her whole body was hot, but her hands, where they were holding David's head, were radiating heat. Jack would also remember later that the whole scene shifted, like a computer screen doing a degaussing reset. Everything shimmied and then returned to normal.

Laura bowed her head and said simply, "Thank you Yahveh!" and then she sat back and folded her hands into her lap and was quiet. Jack looked at David's face to find him looking back with a confused stare. He looked up at Sarah and said in a clear and strong voice, "What is going on?"

Sarah's tears of joy fell on his face and she grinned like a kid with a credit card in a candy store. She bent down and kissed David's forehead. He reached up and caressed the side of her face. Then, gently pushing her back, he sat up and looked around. Shaking his head he spoke in Hebrew to one of the security team who was watching the mall area with his weapon in hand. Judah Marriz wasn't at all sure what had just happened and couldn't answer his superior's question.

Turning to Sarah, David frowned, and asked again in Hebrew. "What happened? What is going on? Why doesn't someone answer me?"

Sarah just sat there on the sidewalk, weeping and smiling. Laura was quietly praying.

Jack got to his feet and offered his hand to David. Helping the agent to his feet and pointing at the dead terrorist, Jack said simply, "That man was going to shoot Laura, or Sarah. You saved them by pushing them out of the line of fire. He shot you instead, twice." He watched as David felt his chest and didn't find any damage. Puzzled, he looked back at Jack. Jack put his hand on David's shoulder and with a look of truth and sincerity mixed with happiness said, "He killed you, but God healed you and brought you back to life."

David looked at the blood on his clothes, the blood covering Sarah's hands and skirt. He looked at the dead man with the pistol lying nearby. He undid his shirt and looked at his chest and found nothing unusual. Musing under his breath he stuck his fingers through each of the holes in his shirt. He carefully replayed events in his mind and then, fainted. Jack saw him start to go and grabbed him to keep him from falling. He looked at Judah and said, "Let's get him back to your headquarters."

As Judah and another agent took David's unconscious form from Jack he shook his head, "No, we need to get him to a hospital!"

Sarah came over and spoke to the man in Hebrew and showed him David's chest. Looking relieved and confused at the same time Judah nodded agreement. David recovered somewhat. Then, as a group, they went down the walk leaving one man there to deal with the authorities who were quickly arriving.

When they exited the covered mall walkway into the parking lot Sarah felt it was like the sky was rejoicing. It was a bright, shiny, clear day with only a few clouds and a wonderful feeling in the air. Sarah had never felt so alive and full of happiness at the resurrection of her friend. Her whole body vibrated with joy.

David had recovered enough to be walking on his own with help from Judah. Mark came up behind Sarah and smiled at her when she looked back at him over her shoulder. Smiling back, Sarah stopped suddenly and turned around. Caught off guard, Mark almost collided with her. She stepped against him, put her hands behind his head and pulled his head down. She then kissed him passionately on the lips.

Seeing this, Laura smiled and put her arm around Jack's waist and kept them walking.

Mark didn't break the embrace until they were both finished kissing each other. Then he stepped back and asked, "What was that for?"

She smiled, "Because I wanted to, and because you wanted to. Also, I've got to spread some of the joy in me around before I burst." She looked at Mark and with a little grin, held out her hand. "And I couldn't think of anyone else I'd rather share it with."

The invitation was there along with the future complications, but Mark went with his heart and reached out and took Sarah's hand in his. They turned and ran to catch up with the others. As they jogged he mentioned, "I see you're not limping anymore."

Sarah stopped and looked perplexed. She reached down and pulled her bloody skirt up next to her left leg. She reached down with her other hand and pulled the bandaging from her leg. Letting her skirt fall back into place she looked at Mark with wonderment in her eyes. She beamed as she whispered, "There's no wound, and I don't even have a scar!"

Mark silently thanked God from the bottom of his heart.

Later that evening Sarah cornered Laura and thanked her for praying for David. Laura didn't avert her eyes when she told Sarah that she was only doing what the Lord had commanded her to do. Sarah hugged Laura again and complimented her on her command of the Hebrew language.

Confused, Laura frowned and said, "I don't know any Hebrew at all."

Sarah stared at her for a few seconds and then waved Jack over to them. She looked at Laura while she asked Jack, "Didn't you hear Laura speaking perfect Hebrew while she was praying for David?"

Jack shook his head. "No, she was praying in English."

Judah, who had wandered over to their group, spoke up. "I grew up in a small town in Southern Lebanon and I heard her speaking flawless Lebanese."

Everyone just looked at everyone else.

Laura said, "I need to sit down."

CHAPTER FIVE

The next morning the team reconvened in the same conference room they had met at before. While they waited for David to arrive they bounced around ideas concerning the soft probe of the Software Company that Jack and Laura were about to attempt.

Mark commented, "If they have "made" you, you two won't get by the front desk." Jack thought about that, "Unless they want to bring us in to interrogate us or eliminate us." Laura said, "Ooh! That would not be good!"

Sarah shook her head. "Don't worry about that. If you can gain entry, we will be monitoring your every step and if you get into trouble we will raid the building in a matter of seconds."

Mark said, "I thought you had not been able to get any type of sensors or monitors in there."

Sarah nodded, "True, but these are going in with Jack and Laura."

Laura said, "I hope they don't get blocked or confiscated."

Sarah was about to reply when David strode into the room. After greeting everyone he asked to have a moment alone with Laura. The rest of the team went to the cafeteria to get a soft drink.

David sat down next to Laura and smiled at her. Taking her hand in his he made a short statement. "Laura, I have investigated the event yesterday and have some mutually contradicting evidence and wonder if you can straighten it out?"

Laura prayed quietly in her mind, "Holy Spirit of God, give me the right words for this child of yours. She said to David, "Go ahead and tell me what the problem is. I don't know if I can help, but I will if I can."

David nodded. "According to everyone's testimony I was shot two times in the chest and I died. You agree? Laura nodded quietly now knowing what was coming. David then added, "The physical evidence of the blood and the puncture holes in my clothes agrees with that assessment. Then, why do I live? What happened that reversed the physical damage to my body? I know you, and Sarah, and Jack all say that you prayed to God for my healing, and I was healed, made whole, as it were by the power of God. What I want to understand is 'how did it happen?"

Laura put her fingers over David's mouth to stop him from talking. "David, in God's plan it was not time for you to die. Don't ask me to explain how I knew that. I just 'knew' it. I was starting to pray for you when a power, or force, or the Holy Spirit of God overcame me. I felt this energy that went completely off of the scale as far as I could tell. For an instant I felt that I could see both our world and the world of the supernatural. The next thing I know is that I am sitting on the sidewalk full of awe and loving the Lord in a continual litany of praise and worship. You were like normal and demanding that someone tell you what happened."

She looked carefully at David to see if he understood what she was telling him. "I can tell you this. I have attempted to walk with Yahshua, as many people call Jesus Christ, and have given my life completely to Him to use as He sees fit." She thought for a second. "I am trying to live my life as a vessel for the Holy Spirit. I think during that time He used me and the others as a conduit to restore you because He has future plans for you and your life. I can't give you a scientific description of how it works. It is just a speculation of mine from what I have learned about God. I 'knew' beyond a doubt that it was not your time to die. I don't understand what happened either, but then, I for one, do not believe that God's million-gallon ideas can be understood in our quart-sized brains."

She reached forward and hugged David. With her mouth near his ear she whispered, "I do know that God loves you so much that He reached through us to touch you and change the natural laws of life and death. I can tell you that I have been blessed by your healing." She sat back and watched the expressions move across David's face.

He finally looked at her with tears in his eyes and said, "I am not worthy that YHVH should reach into our world to save me."

Laura shook her head. "No, you are not worthy." When he looked puzzled, she added, "None of us are worthy. But God is worthy and if He deems you worth His attention who are *you* to tell Him that you're not worthy?" She smiled gently and suggested, "Why don't you complete your report with the comment 'the shooting was contravened by an act of God' or 'by forces beyond the scope of this investigation?'"

David nodded and was about to get up. Laura touched his arm and added one more thing, "I spent part of last night thanking the Lord for what He did for you. I was just grateful that I was there to be part of it all."

David smiled a small smile. "Last night, I too was doing a great deal of soul searching. I finally came to accept both the shooting and the miracle although I don't understand the how or why of the second. I realize for the first time that I'm part of something much greater than I am. This is good, very humbling, but very good too."

David smiled at her one more time and rose out of his chair. He walked to the door and opened it. The rest of the team came back in and sat down. David collected his thoughts and started the meeting with, "Well, it seems God Himself wants us to succeed. Therefore, I suggest we get on with the planning."

CHAPTER SIX

As they dressed that afternoon for their attempted entry into the software company, Laura inquired of her husband. "What do you think is so secret that the people behind it would try to kill us at the airport and the mall?"

Jack adjusted his tie and thought about the question. Finally he answered. "According to David and Sarah, the ASF are behind this "shadow organization"." As terrorists, their only goal is the total destabilization and destruction of the Jewish people. Whatever they are doing here is huge and long range. Not just a quick raid or a rocket attack against a kibbutz. So, my guess is that they are mounting something major like a chemical, nuclear, or biological warfare assault and need this company to provide a staging area."

Laura chewed on that for a few seconds. "If the Mossad thinks that the majority of the company is legit now, how are we to determine who are the bad guys?"

Jack chuckled, "Sweetheart, this one is right down your alley. We go in and visit and we let our 'intuition' guide us as to the 'rightness' of everyone we meet. If anyone seems false or seems out of place defensively then we remember who they are and see if David and his people can develop more information on those individuals. My guess is that the people involved in this business of attempting to kill us are going to be knocked off-base by our appearance at this company and will react improperly."

Laura smiled, "My alley? Are you saying women have better sensing capabilities than men for people under stress?"

Jack sat down in the chair to put his shoes on. "Don't tell me you're out of warranty already! I thought sure your 'sensitivity' was good for another half million miles."

"You're dodging the question mister." Laura came back.

Jack got serious. "Yes, I am. But then you could sense that, couldn't you?" He grinned at her. "I think your antennae are fine tuned for spotting dirty work."

She got serious too. "It will be the Holy Spirit that will detect anything, not me. But since we really know who is probably behind all this, we need to cover ourselves in the Blood of Jesus and pray for angels to go with us to protect us."

Jack agreed and they stood there joined in prayer.

Several minutes later there was a knock on the door. Jack answered it and let Sarah into the room. She checked their dress and asked, "Are you guys ready for the big time?" Getting two nods she led them out of the room and eventually into a technical lab area. By the time they were finished they each had two cameras, two separate audio links, and complete processor controlled recording studio on themselves or in Jack's briefcase and Laura's portfolio.

"Why the extra electronics, won't they detect the recording device?" Jack inquired of the chief technician who was wiring them up.

"No, they will see it but it looks like a slightly older model tape recorder and it is in character for you to bring it with you to make notes or dictate correspondence. The reason is because we don't know exactly what type of shielding they may employ in certain parts of the building. When your equipment can't reach us directly it will still be recorded for later examination." He finished his work and tested all the devices and declared them operational.

As they walked from the lab toward the elevator, Laura remarked, "What are the odds that if they want to do us harm it would be in a shielded area? If that is the case, how are you and your people going to know it's time for an emergency raid?"

Sarah looked at her and smiled. "We have one more thing to give you." She handed them both a ballpoint pen. "Push the button down for more than three seconds and throw the pen away from you. I guarantee you that we will get the signal and be in there quickly." But she stopped walking and faced them. "I won't lie to you. You have come to be more than friends to me in the last few weeks, more like my family. There are risks to your going in without immediate backup and unarmed. There is nothing we can do except trust in our judgment that the majority of the business is legitimate and that the group we are after will not attempt to harm you and destroy their cover within the company."

Jack nodded, "That's true and the whole trip will most likely be a waste of time if the players can keep their cool and we don't end up with a group of suspects."

Sarah disagreed, "The video recordings you bring back will give our specialists a wealth of information to work on, especially if we can recognize any of the faces in there. Remember to look at everything and everyone."

Laura said, "But can't your people just photograph everyone entering or leaving the building to get that information?"

"Unfortunately, the business they are in is very secretive and subject to a great deal of corporate espionage and they guard their personnel very carefully. They have a covered and walled parking facility and their cars all have very dark windows. All of the windows of the building are electronically guarded against espionage and they have one of the best chief security officers in the business. A real paranoid professional, we ought to know, we trained him ourselves."

Jack frowned, "An ex-Mossad agent?"

She nodded. "Yes, three years ago they made him an offer he couldn't refuse and since then he has deliberately avoided contact with us so as to not compromise his position with the company."

Laura stepped into the elevator and asked, "If he has almost up-to-date information won't he be able to figure out what our equipment is and what we are up to?"

Sarah smiled a cat-like grin. "No, things have changed a great deal in the last three years and Jacob has not been on our mailing list."

Jack and Laura were driven to a remote garage where they switched into a late model rented Mercedes-Benz. They then drove to the Software Company per their invitation. The invitation had been sent to Jack Malone at Technology Alternatives in Denver, Colorado USA. His was a legitimate company in the United States. In preparation for this event the Mossad had worked Jack's name into the mailing lists through a circuitous machination.

Jack parked above ground where the signs welcomed visitors in three languages. He and Laura walked up the marble stairway to the large glass doors and entered the lobby. Air conditioning kept the temperature at a cool 72 degrees with 10 percent humidity. Jack had a similar arrangement at his company and knew that the A/C was more for the computers than the people. Still, it was nice and refreshing.

They walked to the front desk and presented the invitation and their identifications. It wasn't hard to see the profiling cameras aimed at them through a glass surface behind the guards.

As expected, they were granted access and taken to a small area behind the guard station to wait upon their host. The man that showed up was definitely Jewish. He was at least six foot two inches tall and looked somewhat like an NFL linebacker in build. Smiling, he extended his hand to Jack, "Hello, Mr. Malone, my name is Jacob Kaplan and I want to welcome you and your lovely wife to our company."

Jack managed to act perfectly normal while being surprised by the chief of security. "Thank you very much Mr. Kaplan. It is nice to meet you, but I thought we were supposed to meet with Mr. Greenberg. He suggested this tour and I wanted to talk to him about your software."

The former Mossad agent did a credible act in pretending to stand-in for Mr. Greenberg until he was about to disengage himself due to an urgent phone call. The chitchat was light but definitely an interrogation attempt. Jack began to act irritated, as a normal executive would be at that point. He then thought of a ploy. He looked deliberately at his watch. Smiling grimly, he stated bluntly, "If Mr. Greenberg is occupied then we'll come back at a more convenient time, if we haven't located a better offer by then." He picked up his briefcase and they started back toward the front door. This action had three effects.

The first was to really shake up the Mossad agents watching and listening through their comm. links. They couldn't believe that Jack was walking out on their first chance to see the people in this business. The second effect was to indicate to Jacob Kaplan that Jack and Laura were good business people with a valid offer and being put off here they could find more attention at other companies. The major intent of Jack's feint was to make their wanting to get into the building seem insignificant compared to the business they were there to handle. It was a standard business ploy to capitalize on what you had rather than throw it away. Anyway, Jack wasn't under any compulsion to endanger his wife and himself other than to help Sarah and the Mossad.

As an actual CEO of his own company Jack knew how to behave. He just acted as he would have if he were visiting the company for the stated purposes. This honesty included not having his time wasted. He knew that by apparently being willing to walk away he was cementing his identity and purpose in the mind of the security chief.

Jacob Kaplan also came to a realization that he was apparently jeopardizing a real client and that was not what he was tasked to do. Check people out, yes, drive away potential buyers, no. He had to answer to the CEO and the Board of Directors and this could end up as a black mark on his record. "Typical Americans" he thought, "They think their time is more valuable than anyone else's." But, he felt the very real threat if they walked out.

The security chief politely asked Jack to please wait a few more minutes and he would see if he could hurry Mr. Greenberg up. It was hardly a surprise when Mr. Greenberg appeared immediately after that. The only real result of Jack's implied walkout was an increased use of antacids in the Mossad headquarters building across town.

Jack was well informed on computer software to begin with. Bolstered by the information the Mossad had on the new version of the E Commerce Control software about to be announced he was more than able to play the part the Israeli intelligence service needed him to handle. While considering his 'role' he had come to the conclusion that he liked the company's current software well enough he just might really sign up as the American Distributor.

Their initial offering was a revolutionary, not evolutionary, step in allowing a person, or a company, to completely step out of the real world into the cyber world. No more letters to be filed, no more outside groups to hire to do research or fill labor positions, no more plant overhead. This software, dubbed E-One, allowed a person to fill orders with his own products which were made by someone else and presented JIT (just in time) for the sales. The money exchanged hands over the net, the banking was done over the net, and the new designs were thought up using the entire world as a brain trust. The software presented everything as a virtual office and provided access and business control to everything that was done. The possibilities were endless.

The only possible drawback was that a person lived in cyberland and never really met or talked with anyone else. Oh, you had e-mail, and chat rooms, and meeting rooms. But those were virtual people, not real people.

Right or wrong, this was the way the world commerce was going. One could join in or fall by the wayside to be forgotten immediately. The software had rocketed to the top of the sales charts and was a huge success for the Israeli-based American company. It not only brought hundreds of millions of dollars into Tel Aviv from all over the world, it reaffirmed Israel as a major player in the software world.

The new software they were about to announce was directed more toward the Middle Eastern countries than the industrial West. It was a computer program to manage and conserve water. In the arid desert this was an important thing. This new software would allow a person with one well, or a combine with thousands of acre-feet of water to precisely control the use, recovery, evaporation, and quality of the water they possessed. Even a homeowner in an arid country could save big bucks on their water usage with this package and several hundred dollars worth of water interface control valves.

Guaranteed to pay for itself within the first year of use, the advance orders had threatened to overwhelm the production department's ability to meet new sales upon announcement.

Jack's role with this product called for him to examine the software and the manufacturing facility to determine their ability to supply the American Southwest within the next three months. He noticed that they were still operating in a traditional way instead of using their own software to work through the web, interesting.

Ira Greenberg was an avid software engineering marketing manager with an agenda. Even though he wasn't particularly fond of Americans or Christians per se, he really knew his product and how to make a sale. He was expansive about the capabilities of the new water management software and sat Jack and Laura down at terminals and walked them through all the steps and features of the application. He then took them throughout the buildings many levels and manufacturing labs. They ended their tour in the hospitality suite where deals were consummated. Since the Mossad wanted to make their visit authentic they had authorized two hundred thousand dollars in U.S. currency at a local bank for Jack to draw on in purchasing software. In actuality, they knew they could turn around and sell the software for thirty-percent to fifty-percent more than they paid for it. Therefore, Jack signed a deal for an initial order of two thousand sets of the software at a dealer discounted price of $100, to be delivered in the next ninety days to an address in the U.S. that was really a Mossad safe house.

They walked out of the front doors and drove back to the drop point. Chauffeured back to the headquarters building they surrendered their electronics to the lab and went to find David.

David greeted them and asked what they had discovered during their time at the software company. Jack looked at Laura and summed it up. "Not much, probably nothing. We didn't interface with many people other than the security chief and our marketing contact. We did cover a great deal of the floor plan and were seen by almost everyone in the building. Hopefully your videos will give you something more than we were able to find.

"Possibly, you guys did a great job as penetration agents and we are indebted to you for your efforts. On behalf of my organization, I want to thank you." David looked at his watch. "I guess I'll let you go to a hotel room we've set up as a part of your cover and get some rest. We won't know the results until late tomorrow. There is a chance that the software people will call you for additional sales pitches or to check you out again."

As they walked out to the elevator, Laura leaned against Jack and whispered, "Did we just get let go?"

Imitating David's precise tones Jack said, "Possibly."

CHAPTER SEVEN

A hot wind blew against the hotel windows but the suite the Malones occupied was cool, dry, and boring. After sleeping as much as possible, exercising, and eating and drinking, they had run out of things to do. Calls to David, Sarah, and even Mark had not been returned. Deciding to leave the suite and walk around the city the young couple enjoyed the strange sights and different smells that identified Tel Aviv from any other city in the world. They kept a low profile because they knew that some Israelis treated Christians as a religious cult, and frequently viewed them as a dangerous cult. The propagation of Christian literature or tracts was banned by law and there were repeated attacks on Messianic Synagogues and organizations. Not all Jews mistreated or mistrusted Christians. Most did not consider them at all. Jack knew the general population was no more hostile to them than the majority of Americans were to Arabs in the U.S. He also knew that twenty percent of the Jews weren't religious at all. They were simply not interested in God.

On a whim they decided to take a two-day tour of the northern part of Israel. They called a travel company advertising "English spoken here" and "See Lot's wife!" The tour was interesting and a decided break from the hectic, deadly life they had been living. Of course, there were the reminders of the state of survival mindset. The tour guide was telling them that the northern towns along the Lebanese and Syrian borders could be beautiful. But they needed to use caution because the area is very beautiful but extremely dangerous. Apart from the occasional rocket or terrorist attacks, he said, there may be the odd mine field to worry about. In fact, he told them that there was a general alert on in the area they were in right then. Jack figured he was just making the trip more interesting.

The hot wind was kicking up the sand into a visibility-reducing haze outside their tour bus when they approached the medium-sized town of El Miahm. The road curved near the main street running into the town. As they approached the town proper, Jack grabbed Laura's arm and pointed ahead of the small bus they were on. Three masked gunmen had just stopped a car ahead of them and ran up to it. As they watched, one of the men raised his rifle and fired into the driver's window. The other two men pulled the back door open and pulled two small children out of the back seat. As they did it, the other back door opened up and two more small kids, one boy and one girl jumped out of the car and ran for the dunes set back from the side of the road away from the town.

A young woman more or less fell out of the right hand side of the car as the bus slid to a halt a hundred feet from the back end of the car. Two of the attackers each grabbed one of the young girls they had pulled from the car and ran down the road toward the town. The third one aimed his rifle at the bus and fired all twenty rounds in his magazine. He wasn't a very good shot and only five or six of the rounds hit the bus. Those stared the windshield or holed it. Two of the rounds impacted on the seats in front of Jack and Laura and two more went through the roof of the bus. The third attacker then turned and ran toward the town.

The driver was on the floor and he looked at Jack and said, "See! Didn't I tell you that it was dangerous around here?"

Both Jack and Laura heard the Lord tell them, "Help my children."

The wind storm was picking up strength and starting to block out the sun as the two Americans left the bus against the advice of the driver. The sky was an ugly gray green and it was almost as if it was dusk already, judging by the dimness of the light. Laura headed for the woman on the ground near the car. Jack took off running after the three terrorists with the young girls.

As Laura reached the woman on the ground she came to a halt. The woman rose to her knees and screamed at the two children running into the sandy dunes. The children stopped where they were and turned to listen to the woman. The pitiful cry that came from the woman spoke volumes of her heartbreak and her loss. Out in the field the children were crying but sitting still.

Not speaking Hebrew, Laura knelt down next to the woman and put her hand on the woman's shoulder in a show of silent support. The woman turned to her and spoke rapidly. Seeing a lack of comprehension on Laura's face she sat down on the road and began to cry even harder. The bus driver came up behind Laura and spoke to the woman in Hebrew. She looked at him and talked rapidly again while gesturing at the two children in the dunes and at the car. The bus driver translated it for Laura. "She said that her husband was just killed and two of her children were taken. Her other two children are lost in the field and she can't get them back."

Laura didn't understand. "Why are they lost and why can't she get them back?" The wind almost tore the words away but the driver heard them. "Because they are deep into a mine field, don't you see the flags and the warning signs?"

Looking around, Laura noticed for the first time the bright red flags and a sign that read in three languages, "Active Mine Field - Do Not Enter". Her heart leaped into her throat to realize that the two small children had run almost four hundred feet into the mine field and even though they hadn't set off a mine on the way in, they were certain to if they tried to make it back.

The woman was wailing and the driver shook his head. "She said that her little boy, Moses, told her that when he sat down something went "click" under him. She told him not to move a muscle."

Laura began to pray.

CHAPTER EIGHT

Jack's long legs ate up the distance between the bus and the edge of the town. He ran into the area between buildings as the darkness closed in due to the wind storm. His pants legs and his shirt snapped in the gusts of wind and the sand made him squint to keep from being blinded. The farther into the town he went the darker it got. It seemed that night had fallen and the blowing sand made it even harder to see a full block.

By the time he reached the first cross street, he had lost the terrorists and the kids. He came to a stop and listened carefully. To his left he heard a child yell in defiance or pain. Having no options he turned and headed in that direction while he asked the Holy Spirit to guide him. There were no street lights that were working, if there were any at all. Realizing that it was now a cat-and-mouse game, where he could be the hunted as well as the hunter, Jack reverted to his Ninja training. He pulled the wide collar of his dark blue jacket over his white shirt effectively hiding the shirt and his chest and throat. He wore this type of clothing out of habit and it seemed that it was a good habit at this point. Seeing a black cloth blowing in the breeze where it had become caught on a railing, he grabbed it and wound it around his head, neck and face. The only thing showing now was his eyes. He pulled out a set of black, driver's gloves and put them on. He had just rendered himself almost invisible to normal eyesight at night. Of course, it wouldn't help at all if they had any night-vision capability. Sliding into the shadows of the buildings in the dim light, he disappeared as he tracked the three attackers.

Stopping every few feet to listen, he continued to follow the slight clues of a child's voice and talking in Arabic. As he reached the third cross street to the left of the main street he caught a glimpse of something moving ahead of him. Sliding up to the side of the buildings on his left he moved toward the place he had seen the movement.

If anything, the wind got worse and the ability to see was even more hampered by the sand, the wind, and the darkness. On the plus side, Jack knew that the attackers couldn't hear him coming and probably couldn't see him any better than he could see them.

Next to the street, on his left, Jack saw a small, one-story business building. The building was shuttered tight and closed. In fact, it looked like it had been closed for some time judging by the trash collected in the window sills and by the front door. Seeing a low stone wall next to the building, Jack quickly pulled himself up to the top of the wall and jumped to the top of the building, staying low, he crab-walked toward the far end of the roof. When he was almost at the end of the roof, he got down in a prone position and crawled the final few feet and peered over the end of the building.

Next to the building was the next cross street and something like a small park setting. Thirty feet away from where he was lying he saw two of the armed men squatting down behind a small group of hedges. He couldn't see the third man though. He saw the two small girls, probably about three to five years old, sitting on the ground next to the two men. Both of the men held their Kalashnikovs at the ready and were peering over the hedge toward the corner of the building he was on.

Creeping slowly backward, Jack moved far enough away from the edge of the roof overlooking the terrorists that he could duck walk his way to the back of the building's roof and creep forward toward the street again. This time he was twenty feet closer to the two men in the hedges. But, he could also see the street below the position he had been in. The third man was hidden there, obviously waiting on whatever pursuit would be following them. He had his rifle aimed down the street that Jack had been on. At that point Jack realized it was more than just a fortunate way the wall and the roof had jumped into his vision back then.

Knowing that they wouldn't wait here forever, he decided he had to take the back guys first to protect the girls. Working his way back quietly, he found a place where he could jump to the ground without being seen. Jumping lightly in the gloom he almost turned his ankle on a piece of wood laying unseen on the ground where he jumped. The only thing that saved him was his excellent physical condition and the years of training in martial arts.

He quickly crept around another small building and approached the hedges from the rear. As he got close he could smell the men before he could see them or hear them. There was an unwashed smell mingled with a spicy, middle-eastern odor. He was about to go around the hedge when he sensed a movement to his right and in front of his position. Freezing his movement, he let himself become one with the ground and the shadows.

The third man appeared out of the haze and stepped on the ground less than fifteen inches from Jack's gloved hand and quietly spoke in Arabic to the other two men. A whispered conversation took place which ended with the third man returning to his post at the street corner, twenty-five feet from the hedges.

Risking a quick peek, Jack fixed the positions of the other two men in his mind. After one more check on the third man he made his move. Coming out of the darkness he was only one more silently shifting shadow.

Sensing something, the man nearest to him turned toward him and started to swing his rifle barrel that way, too. He never got the chance. Jack struck him in the throat with a full-power knuckle punch. The man's larynx collapsed under the punch and caused the man to drop his rifle and grab at his throat. It didn't help him and he quickly passed out from the lack of oxygen.

The second man inexplicably turned the other direction, apparently sensing something coming from the other side. Still moving quickly, Jack swung his right fist in a big, vertical circle and smashed a hammer-fist at the back of the second man's neck. He had put all his power into the blow so that he would disable the man quickly and protect the girls. There was a subtle "crunch" and the man sank to the ground. Jack knew what the noise meant. The L7 vertebra was severed and the man would join his partner in never seeing the morning light.

His swift attack was over before the two girls noticed him at all. He smiled at them and then realized his face was covered. Hearing a noise outside the hedge he reached down and frisked the first man. Finding a small curved dagger sheathed on the terrorist's belt, he pulled the dagger free and turned to the opening he had just came through. Pulling his arm up and back and holding the dagger by the blade, he was ready as the third man came around the end of the hedge. He threw the blade at the man as he appeared. The unfamiliar knife flew a little high and struck the third man in the middle of his forehead. The force the knife was thrown with was sufficient to drive the point of the knife out the back of the man's head. This one dropped like a string-less puppet without a sound.

Jack turned around and grabbed both the girls and quickly headed back toward the street. He had gotten two blocks in the gloom when he heard a shout behind him. He took off running toward the main street as fast as he could go. The shouting behind him told him that more than several people were chasing him. While he was a fast runner he was hampered by the two girls and the group behind him was quickly catching up. A shot grazed his right arm and stung him. That slowed his pace even further and he realized that he was going to have to turn and fight.

CHAPTER NINE

As Laura prayed she felt a conviction from the Lord that she should rescue the two children. She thought of the mine field and asked, "How can I do that, Lord?"

The blessed peace of God came over her spirit and mind. She clearly heard, *"Do you trust me, Laura?"* Her answer was the same as it had been lately, "Completely Lord. My body, my life, everything I am or have are yours. What will you have me do?"

The Lord raised her eyes to the pitiful sight of the two children she could barely see in the gloom. They sat there in the middle of more danger than they could conceive of, sobbing in fear. The Lord said to Laura, *"Go get them."*

Laura stood up and walked to the edge of the area marked as the mine field. Quite a few more people had stopped and come to see what was happening in the hot blowing darkness. One of the men put his hand out to stop her progress and pointed at the mine field and shook his head.

Laura looked at the man for a few seconds and then smiled and patted his hand. She didn't speak Hebrew but her attitude told the man that she knew about the mine field and it would be all right. She lifted his hand off of her arm and stepped into the sand at the side of the road. There was a collective gasp from the crowd as she started to walk directly toward the children. She knew the Lord would protect her and she walked with confidence. Several times she felt her feet move to one side or the other from where she had aimed them. It made her look a little drunk as she sort of staggered along, but the movement wasn't so great that she broke her stride.

As she approached the position where the children were, her attention was drawn to a large, flat rock. Understanding what the Lord wanted her to do, she stopped, stooped, and picked up the rock. The rock had to weigh at least forty pounds and it made her feet sink into the sand. She pulled the rock to her chest and started walking up the dune to where the two kids sat, wide-eyed, watching her.

Reaching the kids, she smiled a big smile. They both looked at her as if she was an angel. Stepping over to the boy she lowered the rock to the ground behind him and slid it under him carefully. He raised himself up as the rock replaced his weight on the trigger of the land mine. When the rock was in place she took his hand and had him step away from the rock.

Because she didn't know the extent of the Lord's coverage for the number of feet involved, she picked both of the children up and held them on her hips with an arm around each one.

She turned around and started to walk back to the road. The kids were still so amazed that she had come out to them without setting off a mine they could only hug her and hang on.

Again her feet danced to a different tune and she semi-staggered her way back to the road. As she stepped out of the mine field she handed the kids to their mother. All three of them collapsed into a hugging, crying bundle.

Laura smiled at the sight, then her eyes came up and she saw the shape of the driver of the car slumped over the wheel. That took a lot of the happiness out of the reunion for her.

People crowded around her and were asking all kinds of questions. Since most of them were Arabic or Hebrew she could only smile and shake her head. The bus driver came up and bowed to her. He said, "They're all congratulating you on saving the children and asking how you were able to do it."

Then one important-looking, well-dressed man stepped in front of her and made a large declarative statement. The rest of the crowd stopped talking and looked at Laura. The driver shook his head in the gloom surrounding the vehicles and the people. "He says that he is pretty sure that there are no mines in this field and the signs are false to keep people on the road. Otherwise he says, how could you do what you did?"

Laura turned to the bus driver and said, "Tell the "gentleman" that I am a servant of the Lord Yahshua who protected me from the mines. Psalms 119:105 says that the Lord's word is a lamp unto my feet, and a light unto my path. The Lord Yahshua guides my footsteps, even in a mine field. If this man wants to debate that, then have him prove his statement and walk out there himself."

The driver repeated the words to the pompous man who inflated his size rather like a pigeon and sputtered some explanation or denial. Not caring about him or the crowd, Laura turned to see if she could find Jack when a hand on her arm stopped her. She turned to see the mother with her two kids next to her. The mother stepped forward and hugged her and kissed her on the cheek. She smiled and stepped back. That was an acceptable "thank you" for Laura.

It seemed to have gotten darker since she had given the kids to their mother and she almost had to feel her way back to the bus to get out of the wind and the sand. Her prayer of thankfulness to God for helping her save the children was followed quickly by one for Jack's protection and quick return. She felt the Lord told her, *See, you trusted me and I protected you. I will also protect your husband.*" Laura let her concern for Jack evaporate in the peace of the Lord.

The bus driver was defending Laura's actions and badgering the man who thought that there weren't any mines to prove it by walking out there himself. The man finally turned and hurried away.

CHAPTER TEN

Just as he got ready to stop and turn, Jack was blinded by a light from directly in front of him. A voice in Arabic, amplified greatly, rang out and Jack slid to a halt. Now, he knew the crowd would be upon him. He looked back and saw the dozen or so men stopped in their tracks. Their faces showed fear, rather than anger, very clearly in the bright light.

Jack turned around and saw three more lights come on behind the first one. At first, what he was seeing didn't make sense in the dark. Then it came together for him and he realized he was standing ten feet in front of an Israeli main battle tank. He could see soldiers moving around behind the lights. "Boy" he thought, "Just in the nick of time!" The two girls were shielding their eyes from the light. Two soldiers appeared out of the light and took the girls from Jack's hands. Two other soldiers stepped up to him. One of them held his assault rifle pointed at Jack while the other one handcuffed him with plastic riot cuffs.

Confused as to their actions, it suddenly dawned on Jack that what he knew, they didn't and what they thought was anything but the truth. Looking at it from their viewpoint he could understand his treatment. They hear a crowd chasing someone. They stop them and see a crowd chasing a masked man with two children in his arms. It's obvious that he has stolen the children from the people and was trying to escape.

The two soldiers walked him backwards to the side of the road and one of the tanks pulled around the first one and moved toward the people who began to back pedal and head away from the tank.

Jack said to one of the two soldiers, "I am an American citizen and I was rescuing those girls from terrorists."

Hearing his English, one of the two men unwound the cloth from Jack's head. He studied Jack's face and then looked at his partner. The partner shrugged and pulled out a small caliber pistol from a holster. The first man forced Jack to his knees and pushed his head to the ground.

Jack realized that talking to these soldiers wasn't going to do any good. They were getting ready to execute him without a trial or even listening to his side of the story. He felt sadness well up inside of him for Laura who would have to carry on without him. He prayed that Father Yahveh would protect him and if necessary, take his spirit to heaven to live with Him.

The soldier with the pistol was stepping behind him when Jack clearly heard the Lord say, *"Arise, and don't give in to the enemy."* Jack tucked his head below his chest and did a quick forward roll. This caught the soldiers completely by surprise. As he was rolling he kicked back with both feet and knocked both men down. Completing his roll Jack came to his feet and turned to face the men still falling to the ground.

Another soldier saw Jack's action and flipped his selector switch to full automatic on his Galil assault rifle. He had a clear fire lane and proceeded to fire the full twenty rounds in the magazine at Jack. The impact of dozens of bullets caused a lot of sand behind Jack to explode into the air.

Jack glared at the soldier that had fired at him. The young soldier was hurriedly putting a new magazine into his rifle when an authoritative voice rang out. All of the soldiers came to attention with their rifles at port arms. A Colonel in the IDF walked into the light and looked at Jack and the cloud of dust still rising behind him from the impact of the bullets. The Colonel told the men to disperse and they faded away. He looked at Jack and took out a combat knife and walked over to where Jack stood. In English he said, "Turn around, please."

Asking the Lord if he should, Jack got encouragement and turned around. The Colonel cut the handcuffs off of Jack's wrists and put his knife away. Jack turned around and rubbed his wrists. He and the Colonel stared at each other for several seconds before Jack suggested that the officer had some explaining to do. Either that, or the Palestinian newscasters were right in declaring the IDF a killer force that doesn't care about law or procedure and Jack would see that America brought that fact to the world's attention.

The Colonel took on a grim look and said, "Unfortunately, fighting against people who don't obey any laws and kill whenever and whoever they want to develops a callousness that eventually resembles the horror you are fighting against. If you follow the full letter of the law and try to arrest and try every terrorist, you end up being overwhelmed by your own laws. They win by default. While we do allow some latitude in dealing with obvious terrorists, such as masked men who steal children, there is a hearing and a decision before an execution. You're right, these men were wrong and they will be punished for their actions. Just so you don't think it will be a "whitewash" as you Americans call it, these two will be demoted and returned for remedial training. Their tours will be extended to make up for their "training" time and they will be watched from now on. If they try to take the law into their own hands again, they face hard time in prison."

Jack was still in his own form of shock over not dying, "Okay, okay, I know it didn't look good but I really was rescuing those children from three men that took them out of a car about thirty minutes ago."

The Colonel was still staring at Jack. "Could I ask how you were able to prevent any of those bullets that might have hit you from hurting you? Is this some new CIA technology that we don't know about yet?"

Still irritated by the callous treatment, Jack shook his head. "Colonel, I am a servant of the Lord Yahshua and I can only guess that He wasn't ready for me to die this time. His technology is way ahead of ours."

The Colonel shook his head. "I don't know if I can report that your God saved you and still keep my rank."

Jack thought for a few seconds, "He's your God too, whether you want to admit it or not. Anyway, why don't you just forget the matter as far as a report goes and do your discipline based on your observation of the two men and their attitudes and actions, before they again do something stupid like executing someone without ascertaining the facts?"

The Colonel slowly nodded his head. "But, I still don't understand it."

Jack smiled at him. "Just postulate a living God who is interested in everything we do and is involved in everyone's life because He loves everyone so much. Then do the math. It's actually quite simple."

The Colonel took out a digital voice recorder and asked Jack to tell him what had happened in his own words. Jack described the attack on the car and his chase of the three men. He ended with, "I was able to subdue the men and get the girls and leave. Then the crowd appeared and started chasing me, until the Israeli Defense Force intercepted us. You know the rest."

The young Colonel studied Jack for a few seconds. "You "subdued" them? Can you describe them and tell me which way they headed?"

Jack smiled a bleak smile. "Sure." As he described the three men and the robes they were wearing and the weapons they had, the Colonel was nodding. "Yes, yes. We know them quite well in fact. They are all Al Qaeda trained and very fierce warriors. They are suspected in more than a dozen deaths of our soldiers in the last two months. We have been looking for them and if you'll tell me where they were headed we will make a sweep of the town and see if we can collect them."

Jack nodded. "That shouldn't be too hard. You should still find them at that street corner I described. As to where they're headed, it's straight to hell from my view point." Seeing the confusion on the officer's face, Jack added, "They won't bother you anymore. I killed all three of them during the rescue. If you need the particulars, I crushed the throat of the first one, snapped the spine of the second and used one of their daggers to give the third one a fatal splitting headache. He'd be the one lying on his back with a dagger handle sticking out of his forehead."

The Colonel looked at Jack with a new respect. "You said that they each had a Kalashnikov rifle, right?"

Jack smiled that grim smile again, "So?"

There was a bit of commotion and Laura and the girl's mother appeared and there was another reuniting melee. The Colonel settled the group down and started getting more reports. After talking to the officer, Mrs. Jakobson walked over to the Malones. She stood there and looked at Laura and then at Jack. "My name is Iris Jakobson and I owe the two of you four times my life for saving my children for me. I was weak and you were strong for me. I will not forget it, ever. She slowly spelled out an international phone number. Jack memorized it immediately. She came over and pulled Jack's head down and gave him a kiss on the cheek and a hug. Looking up at his face she said, "Thank you, from the bottom of my heart. If you ever need help, remember that number. Help will be there for you."

Laura smiled at the woman, "I didn't know you spoke English."

She shook her head, "At the moment, I forgot I could. Excuse me. I need to get back to the children." Smiling at them both again, she turned and walked back to the four children.

Jack said to Laura, "That's a strong woman." Laura nodded as she watched her with her children."Yes, she is. Considering that she just watched her husband being murdered."

Jack and Laura moved off to one side and talked between themselves. Jack looked at where the dust was still floating in the air. He smiled and said, "You have no idea what just happened to me."

Laura's eyebrow went up a notch. "I doubt that it can top what God just had me do, but I want to hear all about it."

Jack looked at his lovely wife and nodded, "Later, when we have more time." He saw the bus driver waving at them from behind one of the tanks. "I think we're done with this part of the tour. Shall we get back to Tel Aviv?"

CHAPTER ELEVEN

It was early the second night after their tour of the Software Company that they returned to Tel Aviv and the city was ablaze with lights. Tel Aviv is the most modern city in Israel and reminded Jack of a normal U.S. city. After a quiet dinner they decided to return to the hotel and see if there were any messages for them. There was a call from Sarah asking them to call when they got back.

Talking to Sarah they found out that they had missed nothing. Most of the Mossad's work is like that of any intelligence service and really quite boring. The videos of the company were still being analyzed and there was little for her to do at the moment. She asked if she and Mark could join them for a late dinner at the hotel.

It was a comfortable meeting. It was obvious that regardless of what her agency thought of the Malones the four of them were a family bonded together by their mutual experiences in life and death.

Jack and Laura related their adventures on their tour. It took Mark a while to understand the supernatural involvement but Jack was gratified that he did not argue with facts as given. It was also obvious to Jack that Mark believed himself and Laura, implicitly. If they said that Laura walked through a mine field, twice, and Jack hadn't been killed by twenty rifle rounds through his body, okay. He did look at Jack and asked, "Weren't you a little scared when they fired at you?"

Jack thought about it and said, "No, I didn't have the time to react and even though it didn't seem real I was pretty indignant about it. I think the Lord cushioned the whole thing for me."

Their food arrived and everyone sat quietly until the waiter left the table.

While they were eating, Sarah asked Laura in casual conversation if she knew that the Israeli government normally took steps to prevent demonstrations by the Christian teenage underground in Tel Aviv. But, at the urging of the Mossad, It had issued a permit to allow a popular American Christian rock star to perform in the city. This was a considerable allowance since they normally frowned on any type of Christian activities.

Laura hadn't heard about it and asked who the star was. Sarah asked her if she had heard of the Christian Pop Rock star, "ArchAngel Fire". Laura looked up in surprise and elbowed Jack. "She's a star? You're kidding, right?"

Sarah nodded her head. "Really, she is the latest teenage underground sensation here in Israel in the Christian community."

Laura shook her head, "She's Jack's step-sister. We knew she was making waves in the U.S. but didn't know she had made a jump to 'stardom'."

Sarah looked at Jack with interest. "If she's your step-sister, maybe you can get tickets to the concert that the eOne Software Company is putting on next weekend."

Jack shrugged, "I don't know if she has any pull over here, but I can call and ask her."

Sarah stared at them both and laughed, "You really don't know, do you? She's headlining part of the upcoming eOne show. She will be here tomorrow."

It was Jack's turn to shake his head. "Great, my little step-sister is the star for a show given by a company that is implicated in a threat against the entire nation of Israel. That's not a good thing."

Sarah said, "I doubt that she has any idea of what's going on over here or is involved in anything except the concert. She was probably approached by an agency drumming up acts to draw crowds. Because Christian rock is big in the counter culture underground right now, they knew she would be a big hit here. They also knew because she is still new to the industry she wasn't in a position to ask a huge salary, yet still hungry enough to want to do it."

Jack sighed in exasperation. Laura pulled her wallet out of her bedraggled purse and showed Sarah a picture of Christi Steele before she became a "star". A young woman in her early twenties, she had shoulder length blonde hair and an aggressive, attitude judging from her pose in the picture. Her stage name of "ArchAngel Fire" was related to her first big hit of the same name.

Sarah looked at the picture and nodded. "She's very beautiful and that goes a long way with the teens and tweens these days. I really like her singing. It's very energetic with a dance fever back beat. I do hope that she doesn't get in the way of whatever is going on over here." She handed the picture back to Laura and suggested they turn in for the night because tomorrow might be a big day. Everyone agreed and headed for their respective quarters.

CHAPTER TWELVE

While the foursome in Israel was discussing Christi Steele, the object of their talk was standing in a line in Denver, Colorado to get her first-class reservation to fly to Israel. This wasn't what Christi, AKA "ArchAngel Fire", wanted to be doing right then. Her manager told she would get her ticket when she got to the airport. He didn't mention that she would have to do all her own legwork. She had lyrics dancing in her head she desperately wanted to put down in her tablet PC and new melodies kept popping up to entice her, but she was concerned she might forget them by the time this was over!

A tall, full-bodied young woman with good looks and a head full of honey blonde hair, she wasn't even paying any particular attention to her local environment but instead, in her mind, she was already in the Mid-East putting on her first show. The ticket attendant had to call her three times before she became aware that it was her turn at one of the ticket counters. Pulling all of her luggage with her she lifted the majority of it up to the pass-through scale with deceptive ease. She wasn't model thin but she wasn't carrying much excess weight. Her secret was in the weight and physical training she worked at every day.

Getting her round trip ticket and securing it in her purse, she endured the routine lecture on not letting anyone get near her luggage or accepting a package from someone. Walking away from the counter she knew she had over an hour before her flight boarded. Finding a remote seating area in the terminal she sat down and began to write song lyrics.

After a while she got that feeling all women know. Someone was staring at her. She looked up and saw three teenage boys in scruffy clothes and lots of metal stuck through various parts of their anatomy. She had a lot of young fans, but being in the Christian music market, she didn't have many like these. She said a quiet prayer to the

Lord for protection and went back to writing. But, they wouldn't leave well enough alone. They wandered over to where she was sitting alone in the back of the seating area and started making childish sexual comments about her and what they would do if they were all alone. She had almost slipped over the fine line between "ArchAngel" and "Fire", when an airport security man showed up. He ran the boys off and turned to Christi. "I'm sorry, Miss, if they were giving you a rough time. I'll see that they stay away from now on."

She smiled at him and said, "Thank you." Attempting to write some more, she noticed the guard hadn't left. Looking up, she was going to inquire what he needed, when he stepped close to her and took the liberty of running his fingers through her hair. Smiling, he told her, "You know, I'm pretty much in charge around here." Obviously, puffed up by his own image of himself, he was sure this young woman would be thrilled to have a man in uniform interested in her.

Unfortunately, concentrating on her songs she ignored his interest in her, saying, "Do you mind, I'm busy here." It wasn't said with an eye to deflate his ego, but it accomplished that effort very well.

Irritated by her casual dismissal, he grabbed her right bicep and lifted her out of her seat. "You'd better pay attention to m….EYOOOO". He had started to lean on her when pain exploded out of the hand he was holding her with. He dropped his flashlight and grabbed his hand to try to control the pain. She stood there looking at him with an irritated frown on her face.

Cursing, he looked at his hand and the little finger that wasn't going the same direction as the other three fingers. The joint of his little finger was the assembly that was crying out in anguish. Really mad now, his eyes flared and he turned back to the female that had caused this pain. It was obvious that he wanted her to pay for this insult. Starting to move toward her he saw her step toward him and put her hands up on his chest. Then using her full weight and leverage, she thrust both hands, and the taller security guard, powerfully out in front of her. This caused him to fly backward and crash into a table and two chair sections. Everything was knocked out of his way and he fell to the floor. He fell very hard because his feet weren't on the floor at that point. He tried to break his fall but unfortunately he used the hand with the damaged finger and it had no interest in breaking his fall.

Airport tile floors are meant to take a lot of abuse from daily use and are pretty unforgiving when you fall on them. This was no exception. The security guard hit the floor hard enough to knock the wind out of his lungs and his head bounced hard enough he almost passed out. He decided that for the time being he would simply lie there and incur no more damage.

Christi had pulled the man's hand off of her arm by breaking the little finger as she used it as a lever and then used a basic Kung Fu forward shove to get some fighting room. The needle had swung all the way over to "Fire" and "ArchAngel" wasn't involved at this point.

Doing some isometric stretches while she waited for her target to arise, Christi decided to take out some of the irritation she had been feeling about this whole airport thing. This resolution would have been obvious to anyone looking at her face at that time.

Fortunately, for the hapless and clueless guard, he did take a look and decided to take the "ten count" instead or getting up and getting beat even worse.

Two real policemen came over and asked what was going on. Before the guard could make up a story, an airline ticket agent came over and told the police what the guard had done. She had been only ten feet away and was irritated enough for everyone about his behavior. By the time she got done talking the police had secured a statement from Christi and the ticket agent. They handcuffed the security guard and read him his rights, then took him away for treatment and a stint in the Denver County Jail to await trial for misdemeanor assault and battery.

A crowd had gathered by this time and one of the airport management personnel politely, but firmly, escorted Christi to a private lounge. He made apologies for the guard's actions. He was obviously worried about the legal ramifications that could befall his organization if she wanted to complain.

Mollified by the attention and the quiet surroundings, Christi asked just to be left alone until her flight was called. Far from being upset by the action, she had just tapped into a whole new concept for some aggressive Christian rock music and wanted to get the idea in her computer before she lost the theme.

When her flight was called, the airport management made sure she was given a ride to her gate and the attendant was very solicitous as to anything they could do for her before the departure. "Well" She thought, "I wanted service and I did get service. Thank you Lord." She walked in faith as much as possible and asked forgiveness for the rest. She could see God's hand in giving her the desires of her heart.

The rest of the trip to Tel Aviv was uneventful and she managed to catch up on both, a lot of music and a great deal of sleep on the way.

While she slept fitfully on the plane she envisioned her first international concert. This was exciting and would really help her image in the U.S. She thought, "Wow! This is so great, what could go wrong?"

CHAPTER THIRTEEN

As the plane landed in Israel, Christi touched up her makeup and gathered her things for the trip to the hotel. Her itinerary said that there would be someone there to meet her after she pasted through customs.

As she processed through customs, she noticed that everyone there was somewhat business-like and a bit tense. Therefore, she made a point of acting very sober and in control. Something about the serious nature of the security officers and the open display of submachine guns tended to subdue her.

As she finished clearing customs she saw a sign with her stage name on it and made her way through the crowds to the sign. The man holding the sign was a chauffeur from the eOne Software Company. He got her luggage and escorted her to a limousine. "This was more like it", she thought. She was new to the perks offered by the world of music as a "privileged person." She wanted to be humble because she knew in her heart of hearts that her music and popularity came from God, not her greatness. But at the same time it was great to be treated like she expected music "Stars" would be treated.

She watched the city as it flowed past her darkened windows. It seemed calm and pretty. But Christi was neither a blonde "airhead" nor a typical tourist in Israel. She had studied about the land, its people, and its seemingly unending war with its neighbors and its dislike for Christians. Besides that, she had called her step-father Steve Malone and had him fax her some modern CIA appraisals of the present state of Israel. She was aware of the dangers and the forces ranged against the tiny nation. She had really debated whether or not to go. The thing that decided her was a leading from the Lord. He definitely wanted her to go. For some reason she thought of the Apostle Paul and the trips he had made for the Lord in the first century.

As the limousine pulled up to the hotel, a large crowd of more than three hundred teenagers seemed to form out of nowhere. They made way for the limo and she was able to get to the front entrance of the hotel. The driver got out and got her bags while the hotel doorman opened the back door to let her out. As she stepped out the crowd went wild. Screaming and yelling, "ArchAngel Fire!" they surged toward the vehicle.

Taken aback by the unexpected attention, she just stood there smiling for a few seconds. The young people in the crowd were holding out dozens of pads or pieces of paper to get her autograph. Never having gone through anything like this before she made an attempt to sign some of the souvenirs. But the press of the people at the back of the crowd was starting to push the people in front up against her and then, without warning, someone in the crowd reached out and pulled her scarf off of her shoulders. That seemed to incite the rest of the people to try and get some part of her clothing as a souvenir. People started pushing and pulling to get closer to her, which separated her from the doorman and the limo driver. In general, a riot was starting. She was being pushed and grabbed at and slowly overwhelmed. She tried to move but the crowd was all around her and it looked like a sea of hands reaching for her.

Somebody pushed through the crowd and came right up to her. She turned fearful eyes up to see the face and relief flowed through her like a dam breaking. She was never as glad to see anyone as she was her older step-brother, Jack Malone.

Accompanied by several other people he backed the crowd off by sheer physical force. The three adults made a path for her through the crowd to the front door of the hotel.

As happy as she was to be out of the mob, her fans were too new for her to just disappear. She put a hand on Jack's arm, stopping their forward progress as they went up the three steps to the entrance. She turned and waved to the crowd and blew them a kiss. The crowd noise went up like a roar. There were hundreds of "Yeas" and waving. She then turned and went into the hotel. As she disappeared into the hotel there were police whistles being blown and the crowd started to disperse even faster than it formed.

Once inside, she more or less collapsed into Jack's arms and shivered. He held her tight until she shook her head and pulled away. She smiled at him and said, "I don't know how you got here, but I thank God you did. That crowd was getting way out of hand!" She then saw Laura. Christi ran over and hugged her. Laura introduced Christi to Mark Connelly and Sarah Cohen. Mark and Sarah had to attend to business and told Christi they would catch up with her later.

After Jack and Laura had gotten Christi settled in her room, they adjourned to the dining room to talk. As she sipped her drink, Christi studied both her step-brother and his wife. Putting her drink down carefully she asked, "What are you guys doing in Israel, and how did you know to be where I would need you?"

Jack told her that he and Laura were investigating some software that the company she was going to sing for was making. They had heard that she was coming over for the concert and they happened to be staying at the same hotel. So they decided to meet her when she got there. He smiled, "We just happened to be in the right place at the right time. You know a happy coincidence."

Christi made a small face, "We all know that there are no coincidences. They are just God's way of doing miracles anonymously."

They all smiled and Laura asked Christi, "How come your agency didn't provide security for you?"

Christi shook her head, "I really don't know." She smiled a small smile. "I am so new at this concert thing that I didn't think to ask them about it. Also, I would have thought that if there was a crowd, it would have been at the airport rather than the hotel."

Jack shook his head and finished his drink. "No way... Israel frowns on demonstrations at the airport, too many chances for trouble."

Christi nodded. "Well, I guess I had better get hold of the company and find out what my schedule is going to be. My band will be here sometime Thursday." She stopped and thought. "When is Thursday? Is it tomorrow or the day after?"

Laura answered, "Over here it will be the day after tomorrow."

Christi got up to make a phone call to the company. As she walked away Laura looked at Jack with concern. "Do you think that she is going to be in any danger?"

Jack watched Christi using the phone. He thought, "So young and bright." He answered Laura. "I don't know if her job and ours will overlap or not. I certainly hope not."

But, Jack knew in his heart that a certain evil force ran heavily against him and would delight in destroying anyone for whom he cared. There would be a lot of prayer tonight to prevent that very thing.

CHAPTER FOURTEEN

Later that afternoon, Jack walked quietly down the hall of the hotel and knocked on Christi's door. Waiting a minute he knocked again, louder this time. Worried now, he tried the knob but the door was solidly locked. Using the side of his fist he pounded on the door.

He was rewarded with noise and an unlocking of the door. Christi opened the door in slacks and a shirt with one eyebrow up and a questioning look on her face. "Do you need to knock the door down? I was in the bathroom and had the water running."

Jack smiled a rue smile and asked if he could come in. She stepped back from the door and let him enter. Closing and locking the door after him, she came over to the table and sat down. Jack sat down beside her. The table was French provincial with ball and claw legs and was a beautiful deep rosewood color. The whole room was tastefully done and comfortable. He looked around the room and saw sheets of music all over the bed and a CD player with headphones next to it. The afternoon sun was pouring through the two windows in the room. It caused rainbow reflections from the crystal lamps next to the bed and off of some of the CDs on the bed.

Christi reached over and touched his arm. "You know, I may be a bit jet-lagged and not as worldly as you, but even I can tell you're uptight about something around here and I have a feeling that nobody is telling me the whole story. What's going on?"

Jack relaxed a bit in his chair and stretched his long legs out in front of him on the carpet. He steepled his fingers and thought about her question. He had actually planned to warn her to be careful when she was dealing with the software company, but didn't know how to explain his presence or the threat without giving the whole thing away. He considered giving her a modified version of the truth and hoping for the best. That would be best for all around.

So he jumped into it. "Christi, you know that Laura and I have been involved with some pretty hairy stuff in the last two months, right?" She nodded her agreement. "Yeah, Steve told me about some of things going on. General stuff, you know. No names or anything like that. But I thought that you were all finished with it."

Jack laughed a short laugh. It was a bit too loud even in his ears. "No, we're not out of the woods as yet. In fact, searching for lost children resulted in us coming here to Tel Aviv at the Lord's leading." He sat there and tried to find some way to convey the enormity of the possible assault by terrorists, on the people of Tel Aviv, without scaring her half to death. Heck, he didn't even know what the threat was any more than the Mossad did. That gave him an idea.

"Christi" he said. "We were asked here to help investigate a possible terrorist threat against Israel. One of the terrorist groups that are against the Jewish people may be trying to do something here in Tel Aviv." He saw her comprehension and noticed a slight pulling back. He smiled at her to ease her fears. "I've got good news and bad news. Which do you want to hear first?"

She turned her face to the left and looked at him out of the corner of her eyes. "Why don't you give me the good news first? That might make the bad news easier to take."

Jack nodded. "Okay. The good news is that we don't really know if there is a threat or if it is only a rumor designed to rattle the Israelis. It may turn out to be nothing at all." He noticed she did relax somewhat at that.

"The bad news is that the rumor concerns the company you are going to sing for on Saturday." He watched her to see how she took this bit of information. Her lips tightened a bit, but it didn't seem to make much of an impact. Good.

"The reason I want to tell you this is so that you can do your business with them with your eyes open. Don't let on that you know anything. But just keep your wits about you while you're involved with them. Okay?"

She nodded and then asked, "How is it you and Laura got involved with Jewish anti-terrorist activities? This is about as far from a normal Christian walk as anything I've ever heard of in my life."

Jack sat up and leaned his elbows on his knees. "Actually, it is in the service of the Lord that we are here. I don't know how much your step-dad told you about the things that went on in Denver a while back, but Laura and I have been given a task by the Lord that led both Laura and me to salvation in Jesus, and an extremely active role in spiritual warfare in this world."

Christi watched him as he spoke, judging the truth of his words and she could find no falsehood in his statements.

Jack continued. "Satan wants what the Lord has entrusted to us and is willing to do anything to get it. Believe me when I tell you I have been in the same room with a major demon and the presence and power of the Lord Jesus at the same time. It is not a thing you go through and just walk off and forget. Since then the Lord has led us into many strange and dangerous situations but has stood beside us all the way." Jack looked at her to see if she was getting all this. She was.

Christi waved her hands in the air. "Okay, I believe you and I will do as you say. Just don't interfere with my music or my presentation at the concert, please, please, please!"

Jack agreed and got up to leave with the admonition that she be careful. She agreed to and asked one last question. "What was it that the Lord 'entrusted' to you?"

Jack unlocked the door and opened it. He looked at her for a second and simply said, "One of the nails they crucified Christ with." As he turned to go he saw an incredulous look on her face until the door closed between them. He left with the knowledge that she now knew enough to be careful and not so much as to be scared.

Back in her room Christi shook her head and thought "Wow, Lord, is that true about the nail?" She felt a definite conviction from outside herself. She shook her blonde hair loose and thought, "I've got to see that!"

Thinking back to what Jack had said about a possible terrorist plot, she felt good that he took her into his confidence. After all, he knew that she was going to be in their building for the most part of the next two days didn't he? She would definitely keep her eyes open and see what she could see, very discretely, of course. She was sure she could help her step-brother and his wife in their investigation. She wasn't a detective herself, but if Jack wanted her help it wasn't her place to refuse to do what she could. She smiled to herself. She would be glad to help.

CHAPTER FIFTEEN

Back in his room Jack and Laura felt like they had come to a dead end as far as their activities with the Mossad were concerned. They hadn't heard from David or Sarah, or, come to think of it, even Mark in the last eight hours. Jack walked over to the phone and dialed Mark's room. Not getting an answer, he hung up and stood there looking at the phone while he thought over their options.

Laura came over to him and put her arms around him. "Now isn't this what we have been asking for, some peace and quiet with no emergencies, some private time for just you and me? She snuggled up against Jack and hugged him.

Sensing Laura's need for closeness, he put his arms around her and held her while he kissed her. Her eyes dilated some and she kissed him back. Then she jumped back when the phone rang right next to them.

Jack grabbed the phone like it needed to be severely subdued and yanked the receiver out of the cradle. "Yes? What is it?" he asked rather harshly.

There was a moment of stunned silence on the other end, and then Sarah asked, "Jack? Is everything all right?"

Jack took a deep breath and looked at Laura with a little smile. "Yes, everything is all right Sarah. It's just that the phone startled us. I mean, it hasn't rung in so long I thought it was disconnected."

Sarah said, "Tsk tsk, Jack. Don't be so jumpy. I just called to tell you that David wants to meet here at the building again in about an hour. Can you be here?"

Jack nodded, "Sure, we can be there and he looked at Laura for confirmation. She nodded her head and came over to the phone and held out her hand. Jack gave her the phone and walked over to the window. Life suddenly seemed to have more meaning. He realized that he had missed the action and the on-the-edge tension they had been living with lately.

Looking at his reflection in the window he shook his head, knowing that he would probably regret thinking that thought.

Laura hung up the phone and came over to Jack with a twinkle in her eye. "Mark is with Sarah and I think he has been all the time." She smiled coyly at him. "You know we have an hour until we need to be there."

Down the hall, Christi got a call from her sponsor requesting that she come over so that they could discuss her part in the concert. She was already dressed and ready to go. She checked her appearance in the hall mirror before letting herself out of the room and locking it behind her. She had pulled her long blonde hair up into a bun on her head and put a floppy hat over it. Dark glasses effectively concealed her face and she felt confident that no one would see her get into the company car that would be waiting out front.

She walked briskly out to the car and got into the back.

The driver got her to the entrance of the eOne building without incident. As she walked into the dark glass and chrome building lobby she was greeted by the concert organizer and his staff. Things got so busy that she didn't remember that she was supposed to be keeping her eyes open, until it was almost dark outside and it was time to go back to her hotel. They were going to take her out to dinner and then meet in the lobby of the hotel for further planning after dinner. Her schedule filled up very quickly.

Jack and Laura walked into the conference room three minutes early and found themselves the first to arrive. Laura had a little smile going and Jack knew if he said anything it would be the wrong thing at the moment. She told him that they had some extra time, but he had insisted on being there on time. "Oh well", he thought, "live and learn. Even the New Mossad isn't always on time."

He thought about the reports he had seen, courtesy of Mark, concerning the revamping of the Central Institute and its management. There were significant changes made in the Jewish 'old boy' network that used to run the Mossad. It no longer acted almost independently with no one to answer to, like it had for fifty or so years. The major indiscretions that were made apparent to the public and to the Israeli government by former agents, was no longer condoned and a special group who reported directly to the Prime Minister now had the two-edged sword of power and responsibility. The Mossad had come to a crossroads. It could either conform and be held accountable or cease to exist to make room for a newer group. Dragged, screaming and clawing, from their positions of power and security, many of the highest men in the organization were pensioned off and the newer leadership was not allowed to fund 'black' operations that were unapproved.

The dire predictions that the State of Israel would be left defenseless and at the mercy of foreign powers had slowly died out. The new, streamlined, and more effective group, with people like David heading up the teams, had made a surprising impact around the world with their careful, but confident, no-nonsense work. There were still secret projects and even suspected 'wet' work going on, but they were all approved as a part of the entire national strategy rather than operating on their own. In a sense, when they could stop trying to determine the policies of the country, they got much better at their spy craft.

David strode into the conference room with Mark and Sarah on his heels. Shaking hands with the Malones he sat down and put on his headset. Everyone else took their seats and the lights in the room dimmed. A large screen came down from the ceiling and lit up as scenes from their trip into the software company were shown.

David let the scenes move by to one point and then he stopped the movement. Jack was amazed at the clarity and depth-of-field that the tiny camera had managed to produce. David used a laser pointer and indicated one man in a work smock standing to the left of the view as they had walked down an aisle. "This man's name is Aboud Kamal. He is the third highest ASF 'technician' in the organization. He is Amjad Kaumate's right hand man. Wherever there is evil work to do you will find Amjad Kaumate. Anywhere you find Amjad, you will find Aboud, Amjad points and Aboud kills. Just Aboud's presence is sufficient to indicate that there is a major operation in the works. How either he, Amjad, or both of them managed to get into Israel is hard to understand. Every guard, policeman, and agent knows each man's face and habits." David was obviously upset that these people had penetrated their security.

CHAPTER SIXTEEN

Christi finished listening to her music and put the earphones down on the desk. Rubbing her ears to restore the blood flow she looked at the DVD CD player on the desk. She was really impressed that the company would give her one of the hottest new Techo-gadgets so that she could work with her music and that of many other artists. The expensive player used the new one-inch discs and could be used to record as well as play.

The Sony unit she had been given by the promoter was the absolute top-of-the-line. The new technologies allowed her to program and select any of the four hours of music on the disc in any order she wanted to. She looked at one of the tiny discs that used to be called a single-play size.

The little silver disc didn't look big enough to get one song on it, let alone four hour's worth. Setting the disc down, she got out of her chair and stretched. She decided to get a snack from the machine in the hall she had seen earlier that day. After she left the office she was using, she noticed how quiet it was. She looked at her watch and was surprised to see that it was one in the morning in Israel, already. "That's jet-lag for you," she thought. "I didn't even know that it was getting late."

Walking through the deserted office and to the hall, she checked out her form in the windows to the other offices as she walked by. Tall, full-figured, and definitely attractive to the opposite sex would seem to be the ticket. She reached the metal door leading to the hall and the break room and turned the knob. Walking down the hall to the machine, she heard strange noises coming from a doorway next to her destination. She looked in the doorway and let out a scream.

Two men were using a bar and a knife on a third man who was slumped against the wall and feebly trying to fend off his attackers. There was blood everywhere, especially on the victim. Both men turned their attention to Christi as she screamed. The man with the knife turned away from the victim and advanced on her with the bloody knife held low and ready.

Backing out into the hallway, Christi quickly ran through her options. First, pretend you didn't see anything - too late. Second, run away - too late. Third, call for help - too late. Last, defend yourself. This whole dialog took less than a second. By then the man had stepped into the hall and came directly at her. He reached out to grab her with his left hand while keeping the knife ready to strike with his right. Christi took the reaching hand and used a Jujitsu lock on the wrist. She stepped to her right, away from the knife and cranked hard on the wrist lock. As the man leaned forward to relieve the strain on his wrist, she switched her right hand into a T-bar pressure point against his left elbow. Pushing and twisting simultaneously, she expected the man to drop to the floor, maybe dropping the knife in the process of falling. No such luck. The man opted out to run around her while bent over from the pain and pressure of his arm.

Christi was very good at spatial relationships, which meant that at all times she knew precisely where she was in relationship to everything around her. People that work on a stage need to develop this ability or not work on a stage

As the man tried to outrun her elbow/wrist lock, he was running with his head down to take some of the strain off of his arm. He really thought he could come around fast enough to get out of the hold so he was going full steam when she led him into the metal column head first. He did drop the knife at this point, but followed it to the floor moaning and holding his head.

Christi let go of his arm and grabbed his knife. Stepping back into the break room, she met the man with the metal bar in the middle of the room. The look on his face was fanatical and he swung the metal bar at her with all his might, trying to knock her down.

Leaping nimbly out of the way of the bar Christi came up against one of the vending machines. But instead of following up on his advantage, the glowering man backed out of the break room and discontinued his attack. Christi hurried over to the injured man and bent down to see if he was still breathing. Glancing back, she saw the two men run past the door and down the hall away from the break room.

Thinking quickly, she wiped the handle of the knife off on a paper towel she found lying on the floor, and put the bloody thing onto the floor. She examined the man who was wearing some kind of security outfit. It was so ripped and torn and covered with blood it was hard to tell what it was. She eased the man's head down to the floor and was about to leave to find a phone and call for help when she heard him whisper at her.

She told him, "Lie still, I'm going to get a doctor." He tried to shake his head in the negative but couldn't move it much. He tried to whisper to her again and she bent down and listened carefully.

He slowly put his words together, very carefully as if he knew he only had so many left to give. "I'm Jacob Kaplan, the head of security for this company, but I'm also an agent for the Mossad. Get word to them that the terrorists here have made a binary poison. The first half is in the water of the reservoir and everybody in Tel Aviv is drinking it already. The second part will be in the water this company is going to hand out for free at .. at.. He gave a gasp and fell backward.

Christi looked at him. His eyes were open but he wasn't seeing anything on this Earth anymore. She said a quick prayer to Jesus for his soul and closed his eyes like she had seen them do on television. Taking deep breaths to fight off her nausea, she got up and went to the phone. She didn't know what the number was for the police or the Mossad. Her mind spun in circles and she was about to call the operator when a number she had called earlier jumped into her mind.

Dialing quickly, she waited for an answer, but the automated voice mail came on the line asking her to leave a message. She heard sounds in the hall and knew it probably was not a rescue coming to her aid. Speaking quickly she said, "Jack! I caught two men attacking the head of security for this company, Jacob somebody, in the break room. They killed him, but before he died he told me that they were poisoning Tel Aviv's water with something he called a binary agent. But, he died before he could tell me how. Oh, oh! I think they're coming back and I really need your help. Please!" She started to hang up and remembered something. "Oh yes, the dead guy said he was a Mossad agent. Maybe if you can find them they can help." She hung up the phone and thought about it again. Picking up the receiver, she dialed a bunch of numbers. A phone started to ring somewhere and she hung up. She had remembered how her brother had been able to see who she called by just hitting redial.

Moving back away from the phone and the doorway, she heard obvious sounds of shuffling feet and whispered commands. All at once five men with guns burst into the room. The man she had taken the knife away from was in the lead. He pointed his pistol at her and snarled something in Farsi or Arabic. It didn't matter what words he used, the meaning was clear. He was going to avenge the indignity he had suffered at her hands by shooting her to death.

Christi realized she was about to lose her life and nothing was going to stop it. Suddenly, everything she wanted to do seemed so dear and so poorly lost at the same time. She prayed to God, "Lord, receive my spirit." She closed her eyes and raised her hands in supplication. She felt a deep peace come over her and that the angels of God were very near. She was surprised to realize she was completely content with just going to be with the Lord.

The single gunshot rang out harshly in the small room.

CHAPTER SEVENTEEN

In the afternoon, they watched the video and listened to the Mossad describe the records of the eight men that were identified as being in the ASF. Laura continued to pray that the Lord would keep Christi safe. There were some new developments from sources outside Israel concerning the efforts of the men they had located. Nothing was certain except that whatever they were going to do, it would happen very soon.

Going back to their hotel room they checked their messages and had a voicemail from Christi. She just wanted to tell them that she was all right and that after dinner she was going to work late on her music. She told them all about the DVD player the company had given her, very enthusiastic and upbeat, in other words, normal Christi.

They talked and watched some English broadcast television until about ten-thirty. Mark called and suggested they meet in the lounge to talk. Once there, he laid out all the things that were going on with Sarah and the Mossad. The spider web of information and hints and clues were all coming together. There were indications that the terrorist group had found some heavy-duty scientific help and that they had produced something horrible.

There were signs that whatever was going to happen would be within the next week. Unfortunately, there were also hints that it wasn't going to be Tel Aviv, but the United States, or England, or wherever. One lead led them in the direction of nuclear material smuggled into Tel Aviv and to be detonated in the middle of the city. Another lead said that it would be a biological attack, but there was nothing to indicate where or how.

Mark said that the Mossad was not paying too much attention to the nuclear suggestion because they have some very sophisticated monitoring equipment and there was nothing detected in or around the software company or even in Tel Aviv.

Jack asked Mark, "How did they examine the inside of the building?"

Mark smiled lopsidedly. "You did it for them. One of the devices you were carrying was one of the nuclear particle detectors. It came out clean."

Laura laughed, "Oh, that's great. We didn't have any idea they were worried about an atom bomb."

Mark nodded, "Yeah, I didn't know anything about that either until this afternoon. I guess you can console yourself with the fact that if it was a bomb, it wouldn't have made any difference if you were in the building or at the airport. It would have killed you either way."

Jack looked hard at his friend. "Yeah, there is that."

Mark looked up and appraised the atmosphere. "Look guys, I'm leveling with you on anything we do. We are still the team and it is to that end I am working. We represent the President and the United States of America in this whole thing. I'm sorry if you feel used or left out. I would be there too if I didn't have this connection with Sarah."

Laura smiled and put her hand over Mark's much bigger one. "Don't fret about us. We know where your heart is. How is Sarah? Is this attraction going to last for both of you?"

Mark looked inside his mind before answering. He smiled at Laura and said, "Thank you for asking. I really don't know if what we are sharing is a lifetime thing or less than that. Over the last couple of days I have found myself really seeing things about Sarah that I never noticed and some of them really just take my breath away." He looked somewhat confused. "I mean, its little things like the way her hair smells or how she looks putting on her shoes or how she handles an assault rifle." He shook his head. "Pretty stupid, isn't it?"

Laura laughed a deep laugh and even Jack chuckled a bit. "No, Mark" Laura said. "What you are describing is what love allows you to see, past the mundane things that we all do and to the highlights that make one person special for another person. You're just falling for her that's all. And, it is perfectly all right to show your love by telling her the, quote, sappy, unquote things that you find alluring. She will appreciate it, I assure you." She reached over and poked Jack's arm. "I'm still trying to train this guy in the finer arts, so don't feel you are alone."

Jack raised an eyebrow and glared in good humor at his beautiful wife. He was just glad she thought he was worth training.

Mark took a drink and swirled the liquid in his glass while he formulated his next statement. He looked up at the two people in this world who had become his closest friends. "There are some rough spots that you might help me with if you have the time."

Jack checked his watch, 12:45 a.m. already. He nodded at Mark and sat back to listen.

Mark said, "Sarah is in a strange place with religion right now. She is more than confused about her place in regard to God. No, that's not right. She's very deeply worried about her whole life going against the Messiah, as she was brought up to believe the Jewish view that Jesus was only a prophet and not the true Messiah. She can't get her worldview to jibe with the healing of David two days ago." He sat back and ran his fingers through his bushy black hair.

Sighing deeply he glanced at Laura and turned back to Jack. "She's asking questions I can't answer Jack, and last night I had the weird thought that it would be great if you could have been with us to answer her questions, although that could have been rather embarrassing for everyone at that particular time."

Laura had a small frown and asked Mark. "Mark, you know it's a sin for you two to be having sex without marriage, don't you?"

Mark looked at Laura, with surprise, for a few seconds and then laughed. "Don't worry on that point. She has this 'ring first, bed later' attitude that I think is a direct by-product of her work." He smiled at her, "What I meant by embarrassing was that it would be awkward for us to be billing and cooing with someone else right there. Not that the thought doesn't stay too far from my mind. In fact, I was going to ask you about that. Is there a force trying to get me to sin by having sex with her?"

Jack shook his head, "Probably not, although I can't say for sure. What you need to see is that there are two forces trying to make us like the rest of the world. The first are the devil and his dark imps, but the other is much more insidious and hounds men every waking moment and probably all through sleep, too."

Mark's brow furrowed. Now this was something he could understand and fight against. "What is this force?"

"It's you, yourself. The flesh wants to do fleshly things. If you're following your Bible studies you should be picking up on the fact that when you become a Christian the Holy Spirit makes you a 'new' spirit. This is good. Unfortunately, we're still stuck with the 'old' man. Since the fall, when Adam sinned and gave the keys of the Earth to Satan, everyone is born into a life of sin. You get it whether you want or deserve it. This is one of the hardest things to do as a Christian. Deny the old flesh and stand for the new man and follow Christ's example. I can tell you that desire not to do the ungodly things is a tough battle that has to be won every day."

Jack leaned onto the table and looked Mark in the eye. "The bad news is that you can't win this battle against your old self. The good news is that you can ask Jesus to do the battle for you. He can win the war. So when the feeling comes that wants you to go against God, just ask for help from the Lord. In your mind if you can't say anything out loud. God hears your thoughts. I have seen it in action. The neat thing is that the devil can't hear your thoughts. He can only guess what you are thinking. But he is very good at putting words out of your mouth together with other clues to figuring out what you are doing. But our big guy is bigger than their big guy. Just look for help and ask for it."

Mark sat back and mulled that over. Nodding, he said, "I'll give it a go the next time I get urges to do things that I shouldn't be doing."

He motioned for the waitress to get the bill. "Guys, I think Sarah really needs to talk to both of you about her quandary. If it is all right with you I want to be there myself."

After paying the tab he stood up and said "I'm going to bed now." He smiled at Laura, "Alone, in my room." Everyone laughed at that.

As they got back to their room Jack looked at his watch and saw that the time was almost one-thirty in the morning.

As they got ready for bed, Laura was telling Jack how tired she had gotten in the last little bit. He felt the same way. A good night's sleep would feel great. Laura got into bed and Jack turned off the lights and put his arms around his wife. After several minutes she noticed that his breathing hadn't settled down and she asked him, "What's the matter honey? Can't you get to sleep?"

Jack said, "No I can't, something is nagging at me but I can't put my finger on it." As he lay there he noticed a dim red flashing on the wall above the bed. On, off, on, off. He looked up and saw the message light flashing on the phone. He was tempted to ignore it until tomorrow so that he could stay in bed and he wouldn't disturb Laura's sleep. Then it hit him as to the reason he hadn't been able to go to sleep. Christi hadn't checked in. Of course she couldn't check in because they were in the lounge and she didn't know where they were. This was most likely a call from her telling them that she was back in her room at the hotel.

Something wasn't right. He could feel the incongruence in his spirit. Many times this feeling meant that God wanted him to pray. This time it was something else.

Now the unresolved matters were starting to mount up and he knew his mind wouldn't let him go to sleep until he resolved some of them. Well, the easy one was the phone message. He climbed out of bed and went over to the phone and picked up the receiver. He punched the message button and listened to the message.

"Laura!" Jack said loudly. That brought his wife straight up in bed with wide eyes. "What is it?" she asked. Jack was moving with speed through the room, grabbing clothes and turning on the light. "Christi is in trouble, real trouble this time." He said as he threw on his pants and shirt. He went back to the phone and called Mark. A few seconds after Mark came on the line he hung up. Jack looked to find Laura almost completely dressed and wide awake. He finished putting on his shoes as the urgent knock came at the door. Laura let Mark into the room and replayed the message on the speaker phone.

Christi's fear was obvious in her voice as she put as much information on the voice recorder as possible.

Mark played the message envelope and said, "The call is over forty minutes old, whatever was about to happen has already happened." Sighing deeply he thought for a few seconds and then asked them both, "Didn't Sarah say that the head of security was an "Ex" Mossad agent?"

Jack said, "Don't believe everything Sarah tells you Mark, after all she is a spy and a rather good one at that. Also, she might not even know about the status of Jacob Kaplan because it could be a compartmentalized deep cover."

Mark struck his forehead with his open palm. "Rats, I've been lulled into a false sense of security by these people." He stopped with a pitiful expression on his face and asked, "Do you think Sarah is doing a job on me for the Mossad?"

Jack shook his head. "No, because if she was, it would be a lot more intense and she would have seduced you by now, standard spy stuff, right?"

"Yeah!"

Mark punched in a number and waited. No answer. He punched in a second number and was rewarded by an immediate answer. He asked for Sarah and waited. She came on the line. Mark said, "We have a code red crisis. Christi is in grave danger and she has found out more about the ASF plot than the rest of your people and us together. We'll be there in..." He stopped and looked at his watch. "Twelve minutes. Get us authorized entry by the time we get there. And wake up David and your analysis group!" He hung up without expecting or waiting for a confirmation. He knew Sarah well enough to know that she would get the wheels rolling by the time they got there.

CHAPTER EIGHTEEN

Jack, Laura, and Mark walked into the same conference room they had the first several times. David, Sarah, and three other people were in there all doing different phone conferences or calls.

David clicked off and sat down. He looked expectantly at Jack and Mark and waited to hear what was so important that the whole organization was in a frenzy at two o'clock in the morning.

Jack hooked his handheld audio recorder and the phone tape unit into the communications console in front of his desk with the two leads one of the technicians supplied him. He turned it on and pressed play. Everyone heard Christi's words.

"Jack! I caught two men attacking the head of security for this company, Jacob somebody, in the break room. They killed him, but before he died he told me that they were poisoning Tel Aviv's water with something he called a binary agent, but he died before he could tell me how. Oh, oh! I think they're coming back and I really need your help, Please!" "Oh yes, the dead guy said he was a Mossad agent..." Jack clicked off the recorder.

They had him play it a second time.

One of the analysis team asked the assembly, "What is it they have turned into a 'binary' agent?"

David answered, "Probably typhoid, or one of the other common diseases that are available on the market right now."

Everyone started discussing what it was and what the latest sampling of the Tel Aviv water supply showed. Someone produced a report and after scanning it they could not find anything that looked suspiciously out of the ordinary.

Laura asked David over the hubbub of the conversations, "David, what about Christi? Can you get someone in there to help her?"

David frowned and said that he had already sent that request up the ladder and was waiting on an answer.

Mark said, "What was this about Jacob Kaplan being an active Mossad agent? I thought he was hired away by the software company and that he was an "former" Mossad agent?"

David's frown grew bigger at that. "On that matter you know everything I know. If he was a deep cover plant then it was authorized at a very high level and I wasn't aware of it." He really seemed put-out by the fact that he had to learn about his business from people outside the Mossad.

David's phone activated and he listened for several minutes and then he grew more and more upset as he talked in Hebrew. He mashed down the button to disconnect the call. Now his frown was monumental. He glared at the phone system and turned to Laura. "That was the Head of the Mossad. He just finished talking to the PM about this." David shook his head in disgust. "They have instructed me to take no action regarding Miss Steele because it could cause the ASF to act immediately!"

Jack had to bite his tongue to stop from mentioning the risks and efforts they had made for the Mossad. He knew that David was sidelined by his management and couldn't disobey orders without threatening his career and possibly more than that. He looked at Mark and Laura and got up to leave.

Sarah grabbed Mark's arm and pulled herself up and to his side. "You understand that we can't do anything, right now, don't you?" This was almost a plea from her to Mark. Mark smiled at her and told her, "That's okay Sarah, I know the drill."

David said, "You know I can't condone any action that could jeopardize the situation?" He looked at Mark specifically. Then he smiled. "But if you need anything other than people, I'm sure it can be arranged."

Mark looked at him for a few seconds and returned to his seat. He took a piece of paper and wrote several items on it. After checking it over, he got up and handed the note to

David. "If we can have that to Jack's room in the next thirty minutes it would help.

David nodded to him and then Mark leaned down and kissed Sarah on the cheek. "See you later, spy lady." They both got several angry looks at that.

The three of them left the building and went back to the hotel. Jack asked Mark, "What is it you're planning?"

Mark smiled an ugly smile, more a grimace. "I have a well-developed plan of action to help Christi. We'll go in there, shoot anybody that gets in our way, and get her out. Sound okay to you?"

Jack knew Mark meant exactly what he said. Considering all the special operations missions and smash and grab operations Mark had told them about when he was a U.S. Navy Seal, Jack was quite sure he could pull it off too.

Laura chimed in, "Mark, I know it feels like the Mossad has abandoned us, but they are really caught between a hammer and a hard place in this matter. They want to help but are thinking about the millions of people in Tel Aviv. Our forcing our way into that building and probably killing everyone in sight to save Christi could have some really dire results for the non-combatants in this city."

Mark nodded in agreement. "That's why we need to plan it out and do it so that no one but the bad guys ever knew we were there. It's way past the point of interrupting anything that they would have done to Christi when they found her, but not for long. So I think that we will have to plan on going in there tonight. But I need to get at least two more people and David has to get us the proper equipment. I hope that she is all right and that the additional hour doesn't squander her chances."

Jack knew it would be just a little longer before they could try to help the brave young lady he barely knew. He prayed again for Christi's safety and asked God if it was the right thing to do go after her that night. He wasn't sure if he got an answer to that or not. "Okay, we've got roughly twenty-one minutes to get everything we need together and plan this thing."

Laura said, at least we have a good idea about the floor plan of the building due to our walk-through the other day."

As they rode up in the elevator Mark said, "I know David can get what I ordered and get it delivered to us here in the hotel. What I don't know is where we can get a couple more men we can trust. I'm not going to use local talent because most of them would not care what happened to us as Christians. I also doubt if I can get any orders cut for U.S. military personnel in this short of a time span."

Jack asked him, "Aren't the three of us enough?"

"I don't think so." said Mark. "What I have in mind to take out the dozen or so terrorists will take four people inside the building and one outside to make it work. Worse than that, we need trained soldiers that can follow orders and are on the level of a SEAL's knowledge of tactics." He looked at Jack and Laura and asked them, "Where do I get talent like that in this short time period?"

Laura smiled, "You could ask the Lord for it. He seems to honor requests when you ask Him."

Mark made a wry face and said, "What, pray at this time?"

Laura nodded and said, "Yes, let's pray."

Mark remembered how he was very impressed the other times that God Almighty had taken a hand in their battles. So his prayer for people to help them was made, knowing who he was in Christ and who God was. If it was in God's will for them to succeed and save Christi then he would provide the necessary men and material. He remembered Jack saying, "If God brings you to it, He will bring you through it."

The three of them held hands and prayed. Mark started off, "Lord, You know we need two more men... "

Jack finished the prayer, "all this we pray in Jesus' name. Amen."

The elevator reached their floor and the doors were opening. Jack looked at two men who were waiting to get on the elevator. The first man was bigger than Mark and looked like a weight lifter from the top of his short cropped hair to the bottom of his combat boots. The other man was only a slightly shorter version of the first but dressed impeccably in civilian clothes, but his haircut and stance were definitely military, too.

Laura said, "Craig! Kevin! What are you two doing here?" Everybody started talking at the same time and the elevator doors kept trying to shut until a warning buzzer went off and everyone moved out into the hall. Jack made the introductions. "Mark, this is Craig and Kevin Steele, they're Christi's older brothers."

Laura smiled a big smile, "And, they're both active military." She looked knowingly at Mark and then looked upward. Mark had a look of amazement on his face.

Jack continued, "Guys, this is Mark Connelly, our friend and a former Navy SEAL." Both of the men sized Mark up and decided they liked what they saw.

Craig said, "We found out about Christi performing here in Tel Aviv from Mom and since both of our units were in the area or just off shore, we were able to get leave for the weekend to attend her performance. We were just down at her room and didn't get an answer when we called and knocked. Is she out or just sleeping like a log?" Kevin added, "Like normal in other words."

Jack said, "We are very glad you're here but Christi needs your help badly in a big way right now!. Come on down to our room and let me tell you what's going on."

The five of them went to Jack and Laura's room so that they could fill the young men in on what was happening. Jack then played Christi's phone call for them.

While Jack, Craig, and Kevin listened to the phone call, Mark walked over and said softly to Laura. "Well, God is good. Being her brothers they certainly are motivated to help. Now if they were only SEALs."

Laura looked concerned and said to Mark, "Oh, you don't know, do you? Well, they aren't SEALs but Craig and Kevin are both in Marine Force Recon." Mark's eyes took on a gleam and he smiled a smile that resembled a shark eyeing dinner.

Laura's next comment, that with this operation, Mark might be able to top his SEAL intervention on the cruise ship, sent Mark's memories back in time to that unique assignment.

---------------------------******---------------------------

The SEAL team had been returning from a grueling mission that had just about sucked the life out of everyone. The heavy weapons they had to use had been dropped off over three miles in the wrong direction. This caused them to slug through streams and hack through jungle foliage for almost five miles before they got to their target assignment location. The oppressive humidity and dankness got worse as a drizzle set in over the whole theater of operations. As a team they had pushed themselves way beyond their normal limits to meet their objectives in the time allotted to them.

They managed to reach their objective and set up the heavy weapons within a few minutes of the original plan. But as Mark looked at his team he knew it would be a superhuman effort for them to rally into an effective fire team in the next hour. Even though they were in excellent physical shape and still young enough to recover from tiredness in a reasonable amount of time, they had exerted themselves way beyond the call of duty this time.

Cal Thurman, his strongest man was lying on his back sucking wind and too tired to move. Everyone else was collapsed over logs or tucked into trees with their rifles nearby as they attempted to find a reason to stay awake.

Mark himself was numb from fatigue and sore in a dozen places. He would not let any of the men or women under his command do anything he wasn't willing to do, also. He had shouldered his own gear and weapons as well as an M60 bi-pod mounted machine gun and one full can of ammo for it the entire five miles. Small motes of light danced in his eyes and strange gray shapes drifted through his vision as he sucked in the humid air through his nose and breathed out through his mouth.

Their target below was the intense focus of a multi-team assault. The robbers/terrorists/idiots that had bungled a bank robbery had grabbed two dozen American tourists as hostages and hauled them into the jungle.

Several SEAL teams had been training less than fifty miles away when the action went down and they were tasked with retrieving the hostages and capturing/eliminating the perpetrators.

The three teams had surrounded the bad guys in a depression between three hills. The SEAL teams had the high ground and made a demand of the hostage takers that they release the hostages or stand and deliver in an all-out firefight.

There turned out to be only eleven of the bad guys and they surrendered as soon as they realized the odds against them, out there, in the early gloom of the evening jungle. So Mark's team got the time they needed to recover from the trek, and were fortunate enough to have to haul them out, only three hundred yards, to a clearing where the helicopters set down to extract them.

As the helicopters headed out to sea to their assigned carrier, an urgent red flash communication was passed to Mark in the lead chopper. An unknown number of terrorists had seized an Israeli cruise liner less than twenty miles from their present location. The brass wanted to know if Mark and his team were up to providing backup for a crack team of Israeli troops that were on route to the liner at that moment. Mark looked at his spent troops and asked the question. Since they were only going in as backup they felt they could handle it. Mark sent the third chopper on to the carrier with most of the heavy weapons, along with ten members of the team. He wouldn't need those weapons regardless.

As tired as they were, the prospect of more action galvanized the remaining twenty members, enough that they all started looking out the ports for the liner and the Israeli rescue team. It would be interesting to see how they handled the assignment. Competition exists on all levels for people of this caliber.

The darkness of the night was good cover for the Israeli troops as they slid closer to the liner in two assault boats. Unfortunately, it was also good cover for the terrorists who were watching them with night vision gear from the aft deck of the liner. The two rockets they fired took out both of the Israeli boats in brilliant explosions. One of Mark's team spotted the Israeli troops ditching prior to the explosions. While few injuries resulted from the rockets, the Israeli troops were falling behind rapidly and were effectively eliminated as far as a rescue went.

Mark looked over at his troops and smiled. He grabbed the radio microphone and contacted the carrier. As backup they were going to have to go into action because the first team struck out.

The command word was, "No"! Leave the rescue to the Israelis and don't endanger American troops.

Mark just shook his head and dropped the mic to the deck. "No go, the brass says." he told the team.

Just then one of the squad automatic weapons (SAW) team members signaled for his attention. Picking up his night vision glasses he trained them on the big steamship. The greenish cast did nothing to hide the blood being punched out of the eight people, standing by the rail of the ship, by the bullets from the terrorists who were killing passengers. The mangled bodies fell over the side of the ship into the water and sank quickly out of sight.

Mark increased the magnification on his glasses and watched the killers of innocent people laugh and high-five each other as the blood continued to run on the deck before them.

A fire built inside of him that needed to be let out. He grabbed his CAR15 and checked the magazine load. He then checked for additional magazines in the bandolier and his pistol and knife on his belt. The look on his face was not pleasant. He looked up to find the rest of his team on the helicopter doing exactly what he was. The exhaustion was gone and a fierce determination to extract revenge and prevent more killings radiated out of every man and woman in the rotor craft.

Mark got up and leaned into the cockpit of the helicopter and switched off the radio connecting them to the carrier. At a questioning look from the pilot he said, "The radio was damaged and we couldn't contact them. Go to wave level and approach the ship from the bow. At the last second pull pitch and let us out on the forecastle deck. Got it?"

The pilot pointed at the radio and said "They'll know that it wasn't the truth when they check the radio."

Mark pulled his combat Black Talon fighting knife out of its sheath and slammed it into the radio console. After a few sparks the radio went dead. He smiled at the pilot and returned to checking his weapons.

The pilot looked at the copilot and grinned.

Four minutes later, ten men and women jumped to the deck of the liner and went looking for trouble. It wasn't long in appearing. After a running fire-fight half the length of the deck, the terrorists staged a counter-offensive with ten men on an upper deck, enfilading the SEAL's positions and effectively stopping their advance.

That situation changed suddenly when the second chopper with ten more of Mark's commandos slid in behind the attackers and cut them to bits. The other ten SEALs jumped to the deck and joined up with Mark. Sergeant Mike Allen was leading the second team. He smiled and asked Mark, "Weren't you going to invite us to the party?"

Mark grinned in the near dark at his subordinate and friend, "Didn't want to get anyone in trouble with the brass. My helicopter has a broken radio, so I couldn't hear them tell me not to get involved. What's your excuse?"

Mike was looking into the dark toward the enemy. He held up his right hand and Mark saw the printed circuit board from a helicopter radio. The non-com said. "Ours seemed to quit working about the same time."

Several bullets slammed into the bulkhead behind them and they flattened on the deck. Mike looked at Mark and said, "There are still more of them between us and the passengers. If we shoot our way through, it will be real messy."

Nodding his assent, Mark knew he needed more information. He called up two of his team and sent them crawling forward, enough to lure one of the terrorists away from the rest of them, in an attempt to kill the two soldiers.

One of the team had lowered a rope over the side and slid down to the knot in the bottom of the rope. Two other SEALs swung him back and forth until he reached the rail of the ship ten feet behind the lone remaining terrorist. Grabbing the rail, he vaulted it, and landed almost on top of the gunman. As the terrorist started to turn toward him, the SEAL swung his rifle and knocked the smaller man unconscious with one stroke. The three SEALs quickly pulled the unconscious man with them, and behind a protective motor casing.

Mark quickly brought the man back to his senses with a few slaps to the face. Dazed, but aware, the man tried to get away but was hemmed in by the team members that had brought him there. He tried to put on a brave front with bullets from his own comrades flying by and hitting around him. But he quickly understood his life was only worthwhile if he told them what he knew. He made a deal that he would talk if they wouldn't kill him. Mark agreed with him and spent eight minutes getting the information he needed.

Calling five of the team leaders to him he passed on the information. It seemed that this team of terrorists was about thirty-four strong. There were three leaders and they were representing the "repressed" groups against Israel. They had brought on board eight bombs to blow the bottom out of the ship and had them in position. But they had a problem. Their rescue craft had not shown up. They were terrorists, but not ready to go down with the ship to make their point.

Adding to their problem was the fact that they didn't have anyone who really knew how to set the timers on the bombs.

At that point Mike asked why they brought bombs if they didn't know how to use them. Mark laughed and said, "They had a bomber, but he tried to get friendly with one of the passengers on the aft deck. It seems he got her against the rail and she helped him over it into the sea. Because he hadn't wanted any of the others to know what he was doing with a Jewish girl, they didn't find him missing until just before we showed up. They got the story out of the passengers we just saw killed over there."

"So", Mark continued, "We've taken out eighteen of them." He pointed at the captive, "And Gabby here makes nineteen. That leaves us with about thirteen more of them since they lost one overboard." He had to smile at that. "They have us pinned down up here while the leaders are attempting to set the explosives that will sink the ship and do us all in."

Mark was in his element with the problem. He was a strategist and this called for some unique strategy. He risked a look over the side of the liner as it steamed through the sea. The waves crashed off the ship sixty feet below him and the lighted portholes looked like beacons. "Almost like the light bulb they use in cartoons to indicate a great idea," he thought. He slid back to his men and outlined his plan.

Several of the team kept the terrorists heads down with return fire while six members found a hatchway down to the lower levels of the cruise liner, Six more team members found hidey-holes to duck into near the sides of the deck.

The bright lights turned the deck into daylight and none of the SEALs could cross the deck to the cabin area without exposing themselves to fatal gunfire. Their passivity emboldened the terrorists to press forward and attempt to kill as many of the SEALs as possible. The SEAL team fell back toward the prow of the ship, moving slowly into a smaller and smaller area of the deck as the bows of the ship narrowed.

If any terrorists noticed that there seemed to be fewer soldiers than before, they probably thought they had killed or wounded the others.

Just as the team was about to run out of room, several of them took hits. The captive terrorist saw his chance and ran around the large crane housing, toward his friends. Several of the terrorist shot him thinking it was a trick. Another SEAL was trying to draw a wounded member back into cover and got shot through the arm. Blood was flowing freely and the terrorists knew they had won the day. They surged forward to finish off the team. Then the lights went out.

The team members hiding near the sides already had their night vision glasses in place and didn't give the terrorists a chance to use theirs. The noise of gunfire was immense for a short time. When the smoke drifted away from the front of the ship, there wasn't a terrorist left alive on that part of it. Three team members with medical training stayed with the wounded soldiers while the remaining twelve SEALs on the front deck headed for the inside of the darkened ship with their night vision gear in place.

Mark's thought that the terrorists would most likely only have NV gear for the outside of the ship proved to be accurate. As the majority of his troops moved through the gloom inside the ship, they were able to identify and eliminate the remaining terrorists that were trying to use the passengers as hostages. Four of the specialists were tasked with finding and defusing the eight bombs in the bottom of the ship.

Mark and Mike moved very fast through the ships quarters. As they quietly slipped into a dining room they saw three of the terrorists trying to arrange passengers all around them as shields. It wasn't pitch black because of the emergency lighting, but, in the deep shadows and confusion it was a simple task to slide up to a target struggling to keep his hostages still. After that, a knife or silenced pistol brought their threat to an end, permanently. Most of the passengers didn't even know that the danger was past until later.

After two complete sweeps of the ship with NV gear, Mark had the team members who had shut off the lighting systems, turn the lights back on. There was a brief period of screaming and panic as the passengers found the terrorists in their midst dead, but that passed quickly.

One of the terrorist leaders had been found hiding behind a panel in the pilot house and surrendered when he saw he had no chance against the SEALs. The final count was sixteen dead passengers, who were apparently chosen at random, and executed for being Jewish. Their bodies had been thrown off the ship. Terrorists head count, thirty-eight dead and one live captive. Two of the SEALs were dead and four more sustained serious wounds. All eight of the bombs were defused and left where they were for later disposal.

The team found the Captain and his crew locked up in a forward compartment and released them to handle the ship. Three helicopters arrived with Israeli troops to secure the ship in the event other terrorists were hiding, and to eliminate the bombs and/or booby traps.

Mark's team gathered their dead and wounded and hitched a ride on the Israeli helicopters to the carrier which had been steaming toward the liner. Any celebration over their feat was damped by the loss of their two comrades. Mark was especially depressed because it was his plan that got two of them killed. They knew the risks going in, but still, it stank!

The actual details of the raid were never made public, but the fact that over four hundred passengers owed their lives to a team of American SEALs, who weren't supposed to be there, was not overlooked by the powers that be.

-----------------------******-----------------------

Mark's thought returned to the present time. The planning session went quickly until there was a knock at the door.

CHAPTER NINETEEN

After the slam of sound with the gunshot, Christi was surprised that she could still hear the terrorists talking. She hadn't felt a bullet strike her, so she opened her eyes.

The ugly one that was going to shoot her was arguing with the other man who had been beating the security man. She looked up as powder fell past her face and saw a jagged hole in the acoustic tile above her head. Apparently that was where the shot went.

She noticed that the feeling of peace was still with her and also, the feeling that God was near. She lowered her hands and clasped them, while the argument heated up in front of her. The man with the smoking gun was vehemently demanding something and the other man was denying him with a controlled violence that was scarier because he was controlling it.

The argument came to an end when the apparent leader of the group pointed at the door with his finger and the man with the gun stormed out. The leader motioned for the rest of the men to leave, which they did. He turned his dark gaze on Christi and walked over to a table in the break room and motioned for her to come over and sit down across from him. Figuring that she had nothing to gain by defying him she walked over and sat down.

He looked at her for a minute and then started to talk to her in rather good English. "I am Aboud. You are a very brave young lady. When Achmed was going to shoot you, you didn't cry or plead or anything else. Why is that?"

Christi decided to play along with this slime she had just seen beat a man to death. There was nothing to gain by being weak in this guy's eyes. "I really didn't think that he would shoot me", she said.

The man's eyes opened wider. "Oh, really, well, I am sorry that you came in when you did. We were punishing that man for his unfaithfulness." He brushed off the man's death as insignificant, which to him it probably was.

Christi was getting tired and pointedly asked him, "What now?"

The man said, "You'll see. I stopped Achmed from killing you because I know that you are one of the acts in the concert the day after tomorrow and it would not be politically smart to have an investigation into your disappearance or death at this time. If you will cooperate with us, I will see that no harm befalls you and that you can do your performance and then go home to the United States without any more trouble. We mean you no harm."

Christi tipped her head back and laughed. "You want me to go out on the stage and be lively and animated and pert and happy knowing that I'm supporting a killer? Fat chance."

His face took on a sly look and he called out in Arabic. One of his men came in and brought two sealed bottles of cold water. Aboud handed one to Christi and opened the other one for him. He took a long drink and sat there thinking. Christi didn't want to drink with him but was really thirsty. So she opened hers and drank some. She then capped the bottle and waited for the man to make the next move. Her life hung in the balance and at this point she didn't really want to argue. She was just tired.

Aboud looked at her and said, "I'll make you a deal Miss 'ArchAngel Fire'. I'll let you live if you behave and don't give us any trouble until the concert is over."

Christi looked at him and said, "What makes you think I will be quiet the moment I am out of your control?"

He smiled and pointed at her bottle of water. "Because I've just poisoned you and if you want the antidote you will be quiet until after the concert."

Christi's heart rose up into her throat as she stared at the bottle of water on the table. This was how they were going to get the second part of the poison to everyone in the city! Then she remembered that the murdered man had told her that and she had forgotten it.

Achmed walked back into the room and came over to Aboud. He said something in Arabic and then he looked right at Christi and said, in English "I don't have to kill you now. Our man in Rabal-Cote did it for me in a much nastier way than I could every do." Then he laughed a cruel laugh. Aboud glared at him and rattled off twenty seconds of tongue-lashing that caused Achmed to blanch under his tan. He turned and left quickly.

Aboud mistook her continued silence and pale condition as fear of death. "The poison takes a long time before it begins its work. If you cooperate you will have the antidote in three days and it will neutralize the poison. After that you can tell anybody anything you want to. Do we have a deal?"

Christi nodded in assent. Aboud went to the hall and called three of the men into the room and had them pick up the body and remove it from the break room. He then set one of the others to cleaning up the blood and mess. The last one removed the ceiling tile and replaced it with one from the closet.

While he was doing that, Christi reached into the pocket of her blouse and took out a small bottle of aspirin. Keeping an eye on the men she dumped the aspirin out and quickly filled the bottle with water from the bottle on the table. She put the aspirin bottle back into the pocket and had returned to sitting quietly when Achmed returned. Aboud told her to get up. After she stood, Achmed grabbed her by the arm and pulled her out of the room. "You will go with me and my men and don't give us any trouble, understand?"

She looked in his cruel eyes and said, "You're hurting my arm!"

He looked like he had just lost his patience."And you really hurt my head! Don't worry about a little pain. I assure you that you'll forget about this in the next few hours."

Christi said, "What do you mean?"

The terrorist smiled a nasty smile. "Aboud said we needed you until the day after tomorrow, but that doesn't mean I have to be nice to you. My men are very tense right now and a little diversion will let them blow off some steam." He eyed her body with a calculating eye. "I'm sure you will make a great diversion and still serve our purposes." He grabbed her by the throat and yanked her into the hall and the other men followed.

Christi croaked out a feeble "I won't!" and he let her go. He ran his hands down her body and smiled. "One as young and pretty as you shouldn't want to die so soon." He laughed and the other men laughed with him.

Right then Christi wished that Achmed had shot her.

CHAPTER TWENTY

The quiet Israeli at the door handed Mark several packages and left without saying a word. Mark brought the packages back into the room and opened them up. There were a half-dozen rip-stop nylon black suits and hoods with masks. There were six nine millimeter automatics with sound suppressors and sub-sonic ammunition for each one. There were also six combat knives and a package of building plans with markings on them, some det cord, and miscellaneous other items of death and destruction.

Holding up the silenced pistol Craig looked at Kevin. "Well this certainly fits the motto of our service. "When it absolutely, positively has to be destroyed overnight, the U.S. Marine Corp."

Laura smiled, "That was the old one. I like the new one better. Our job is not to judge the terrorists, that's God's job. Our job is to arrange the meeting, U. S. Marines."

The suits fit the four men reasonably well but Laura had to do some quick tailoring to make the smallest one fit her.

After suiting up, the five of them coordinated their movements and were about to move out when there was another knock at the door. Pulling a pair of pants and a shirt over his black suit, Mark answered the door with his automatic behind the door. The same man handed him another package and said it was from Sarah.

They opened the package to find headset communicators for all of them. Jack looked at Mark, "This will transmit everything we say to the Mossad you know."

Mark nodded his head and held one of the headsets up to the light and studied it carefully. Then he smiled and shrugged his shoulders, "Video too." They all dressed over the suits and headed out for the vehicle they had borrowed from the Mossad.

Stripping off the extra clothes as they reached the target area, they strapped on the weapons. They then exited the vehicle on a deserted side street near the building. Donning their headsets they checked the communications. Standing in a small circle while they checked, Mark looked at the people on the other side of the circle. "David, Sarah, I hope you're getting good audio and video, because you will need to be our backup if everything goes to pot."

Moving out at a trot, they quickly came up to the ramp of the parking structure next to the software company building. Craig held up his hand and everyone dropped to the ground and melted into the shadows. A few seconds later a police car rolled by on the street, passing by without seeing anyone.

Going up the structure to the fourth floor level they eased over against the building and looked around. All was clear so they put the shaped det cord in a rectangle on the wall about three feet from the side of an alarmed entry door. Stepping back Kevin triggered the det cord and with a muffled 'thump' a whole section of the brick facade collapsed into the parking lot. When the dust cleared there was just the interior dry wall leading into a store room facing them. Mark used his combat knife and in less than twenty seconds they had an open access to the building without setting off any alarms.

Laura set to moving the debris off the parking platform and into a gutter while Craig screwed two screws into a piece of canvas they had grabbed from the construction site next to their parking place. That kept the opening from being seen, except by a close examination, at least in the dark. Laura took up a position behind a girder and nodded. The four men entered the building and headed down the darkened hall toward the stairs.

According to the Mossad analysis the terrorists would be using a room on the fifth floor just down from the stairway. As they reached the door, Mark gave them their final instructions. "Remember, don't kill anyone unless you absolutely have to. The Mossad needs as many talking terrorists as possible." He looked at each of the other three men. "On the other hand, remember also, we are dealing with fanatics, most likely Iranian Muslim Shi'ite religious fanatics. Their concept is that it is better to die in battle than to surrender. Got it?" Everyone nodded and there was pre-combat tenseness on everyone's face.

Jack spoke up, "This battle is the Lord's. We are just servants and we need to remember that." He bowed his head and the other three joined him. "Father God, bless us as we attempt to rescue our sister from the enemy. Jesus, cover Christi and each of us with your blood and put your warrior angels on all sides of us during this battle. We give you the glory and honor for this battle. It is in your name we pray all things, Jesus. Amen." The other three men quietly chorused "Amen."

That said, they keyed their comsets and took several deep breaths to mildly hyperventilate themselves for the coming action. Mark turned the handle on the stairway door and opened it silently. He moved out first, with Craig, Kevin, and Jack following in single file. They moved noiselessly down the darkened hall toward a door that showed a light underneath it. As they approached it, Jack heard a sound behind them. As he looked back he saw an elevator light indicating an elevator car was stopping on their floor. He said, "Heads up," and he ran quickly to the other side of the elevator door.

As the door opened one of the terrorists stepped out with pistol in his belt and a box of food in his hands. Jack stepped in behind him and applied a forearm choke to the man's throat. The man dropped the food box and grabbed Jack's arms with both hands, his eyes bugging out in an attempt to get air into his lungs. Jack then drove his left knee into the man's back, breaking his feet free from the floor. He used the full body torque of his rather massive frame to hold the man off the floor. By now the lack of oxygen to his brain caused the man to collapse. Jack laid the man on the floor of the elevator.

Mark had reached the elevator by then and stepped in to check for a pulse at the man's throat. He looked up at Jack and nodded while he relieved the terrorist of his pistol. Using plastic riot cuffs they immobilized his hands behind him and then locked his feet together and to his belt at the back. Then they gagged him.

Standing up, Mark slid the rest of the food into the elevator with his foot and switched the power to the car off. This not only darkened the car but it stranded it on their floor and kept the prisoner there.

Moving back to both sides of the lit door the team each nodded that they were ready. Mark said into the microphone, "Go!"

The door opened inward and in twos the team went in, crouched over with their silenced pistols in their hands. The scene in the room was painted in detail on their minds as they entered.

Two men had just finished tying a struggling Christi onto a table by her hands and feet when they saw the door as it opened. They had pistols in their hands but were expecting their comrade with food.

What they got were four men with pistols and extremely bad attitudes.

Being closest to Christi, Craig shot both of the men before they could use their pistols. Kevin came up against Achmed who was in the process of pulling his knife out of his belt and lunging at the Marine. Kevin shot Achmed in the face twice. Achmed dropped his knife and fell to the floor, dead. At that point Mark told the rest of the terrorists to drop their weapons or die. When Aboud put his pistol on the floor the other men joined him and put down their guns. Suddenly everyone started moving and the room degenerated into chaos. There were still eight clever and vicious terrorists in the room against the four raiders.

It wasn't even close. The training, skill, and focused anger were on the side of the attackers. Christi remembered later that there were almost no words said by either side.

As the terrorists charged, Jack shot one in the chest who was trying to get a hidden pistol out of his belt. In a reflex the terrorist shot himself in the groin, which probably added greatly to his discomfort as he fell to the floor moaning. At the same time two of the terrorists jumped over the couch back to grapple with Jack and Mark.

It became hand-to-hand combat as Mark grabbed his man and smashed his own forehead against the terrorist's face. This broke the man's nose and disoriented him. Mark then used a side judo throw to slam the man to the floor. He then kicked the man in the side of the head and turned back into the room for the next battle.

Jack took his man's leaping attack and redirected his motion with an Aikido movement that ran the man's head directly into the door frame. The combined energy of the man's charge and Jack's throw resulted in a loud "crack-crunch" and a dying terrorist.

Four of the remaining men attacked Jack, Mark, and Craig with knives. Aboud headed for Christi with a knife. He wasn't about to let the woman live to tell about the murder she had seen. Kevin stepped into his path with his pistol held at arm's length. Kevin's appearance suddenly altered Aboud's plans. Before Kevin could shoot, Aboud changed his direction and swept the knife across his body from left to right in an effort to cut down the Marine Force Recon specialist. The large knife hit the barrel of Kevin's pistol and knocked it out of Kevin's grip.

Kevin leaned into the attack and shoved the terrorist's knife hand to his left with his left hand. Stepping into the charging terrorist he brought up his knee with enough force to lift Aboud completely off the floor. Since Aboud was busy bending over from the pain in his groin, Kevin brought his right hand up and over and slammed Aboud's head off of a desk, face first. At that point Aboud lost all interest in Christi, the knife, or consciousness. He collapsed onto the floor as Kevin turned back to the remaining four terrorists.

Jack and Mark had already sent one each of the terrorists to their 'Garden of Delights' while a third one was hastening to follow them at Craig's hands.

The fourth man stepped back to reorganize his attack and paid dearly for backing closer to Kevin. The Marine slapped his cupped hands over the terrorist's ears. The pain was so great that his ear drums burst. The terrorist passed out and dropped like a rock.

Later they would find out that the 'battle' lasted all of twenty-one seconds.

Jack raised Laura on the comset and told her that they had "subdued" the terrorists and that Christi was all right. They would be back down in a few minutes.

After cutting Christi loose from the table and helping her to her feet, Kevin was smothered in Christi's embrace. She yelled, "Oh, God, Kevin! I am so glad to see you!" She looked at Craig and gave him a big hug. She then did the same to Mark and Jack. She looked at Jack and said, "I knew you would get here, but I was beginning to worry a little about your timing."

Jack smiled, "You need to thank God for the timing of everything including your brothers showing up when they did. But I am glad that we got here before the party started." Jack was actually very relieved and continued to thank Jesus for keeping her safe.

Christi looked around at the bodies all over the place. Shaking her head she said, "They really deserved what they got." She suddenly looked excited. "I know what they are going to do to the people of Tel Aviv!" She looked at Jack with wide-eyed concern. "We've got to find the Mossad and give them this information and..." She dug the medicine container out of her pocket. "This is a sample of their poison!"

Jack frowned at her. "How did you get that?"

She smiled, "Well, they gave me some and told me that they had poisoned me." She pointed at the head terrorist. "What Aboud-Jerk didn't know is that I haven't had any of the

Tel Aviv water since I got here, so I only got half of the poison!"

Jack smiled at her and took the sample from her. He didn't say anything but he remembered her drinking a soda in the restaurant with ice cubes probably made from Tel Aviv water in it.

About that time there was a moan from the floor and a retching sound. Everyone looked at Aboud as he got to his knees but continued to react to Kevin's attack. Craig drew his pistol but Mark shook his head. "We can give this one to the Mossad as a gift." He smiled, "I'm sure it will go much worse for him with them than a bullet in the head."

Christi said, "He was the leader and he did keep them from killing me earlier. But he also told the men that it was all right to rape me."

Craig said "Well, then we'd better tie him up." He took his anger out on the leader as he used more than sufficient force as he kicked the kneeling terrorist in the back end hard enough to flip him onto his face.

They used plastic riot cuffs to tie his hands behind him. While the others tied up the few surviving terrorists, Mark professionally frisked Aboud and removed everything from his pockets. Jack stuffed a rag into his mouth and tied another one around his head to hold the first one in his mouth. Christi looked at him with a question on her face.

Jack smiled, "Just in case he has a poison-filled tooth. This way he can't kill himself before the Mossad has a chance to interrogate him."

Mark said, "Yeah, but if he throws up again he'll suffocate." Jack looked at the others and decided that the general attitude was...who cares?

Kevin was leaning back against a wall, looking around. He asked no one in particular, "What are we going to do about the rest of this scum? Leave them for the morning cleaning crew? I doubt that they will have any baggies big enough."

Mark said to no one in particular. "Well?"

They all heard David's voice in their earpieces. "Leave, we will attend to your mess."

Jack said, "You'll find another one alive in the elevator car on this floor."

The team tied up the other two living, but unconscious, terrorists. They took Christi and Aboud and extracted to the parking lot where they picked up Laura. On the way to their car they met a ten-man force of Mossad personnel dressed very similar to them. The leader stopped and shook each one of their hands. He smiled at them and saluted. "We could not have done that any better." High praises indeed, two of the Mossad took Aboud off of their hands with a promise that they would "see to his comfort and well-being." Jack was quite sure they would "see to the comfort and well-being of all four of the surviving terrorists."

CHAPTER TWENTY-ONE

Three hours later Jack woke up to the insistent ringing of the telephone. Picking up the handset, he said, "Hello?"

David was urgent on the other end of the phone. "Jack, Aboud's 'confession' led us to a secret base in Palestine. We just apprehended a microbiologist, a gene scientist who was working for the ASF."

At that precise time Jack wasn't sure he understood what David was telling him or that he really cared. All he wanted to do was get a couple of more hours of sleep. "That's fine David. Congratulations. I'll call you later." He was about to hang up when something in David's voice made him stop and try to focus on what he was saying.

"Jack! Listen to me! You must understand. This is critically important to you and the United States, as well as Israel!"

That cleared a lot of the cobwebs out of Jack's mind. "What did you say about the United States?"

David repeated the information. "Aboud's shadow organization was working inside Tel Aviv, but was directly linked to another ASF group that has been tasked with the same horrific plan they are using here. But they intend to decimate the American people."

He continued, "The ASF acquired the services of this genetic scientist who managed to re-engineer water molecules to be carriers of Creutzfeldt-Jakob disease. Remember, this was the disease that rotted large holes in human brain tissue when the person ate meat tainted by bovine spongiform encephalopathy. You know! Mad Cow disease."

The horror of the plan penetrated the rest of Jack's sleepiness. He listened intently while the Mossad agent continued. "While the Mad Cow disease was controlled and almost completely eliminated, this new diabolical version does not require the eating of meat. Just drinking the water would infect a person. Roughly, four months later people will start dying and by that time millions of people in both nations will be infected with no hope of recovery."

David stopped to take a pull on a can of soda.

Jack had a question at that point, "How does any human being, regardless of their political agenda, do things like this to an innocent population?"

David replied dryly, "The ASF do not consider any Jewish person, or obviously, any American, 'innocent'. They use the same expression that was prevalent in your own old west. The only good Jew is a dead Jew! And, since America backs Israel, they fall under the same heading."

"But how does it work?" Jack threw back at him. Laura stirred in her sleep as they talked.

David sat back and thought for a minute. "I have a doctor working for us who was in the United States in 1991 when the Mad Cow thing happened. Let me get him on a conference call."

Jack waited during the few minutes while David got in touch with his doctor and explained the situation to him in a theoretical form that didn't reveal the extent of the problem. The doctor then described the progress of the disease for them both.

Dr. Jamison Whitley spoke quietly but precisely. "I was involved in a case of the CJD episode. I was working with a team on a man who lived in Utah. He was a Mormon and had been married only four years when he was infected. When I met him, Mr. Elwen was dying of "Creutzfeldt-Jakob Disease" or CJD. CJD is a rare and always fatal neurological disorder that has many different forms. The horrifying condition creeps up on its victims, eating away at the brain, giving it the appearance of a sponge.

"It's a horrible disease! I think that all the governments are fools to ignore it the way they have. They're fools because they still can't tell how to prevent it!"

"The previous summer, John Elwen was a big, strapping man who lived life to its fullest. He hiked, played football and rode his bicycle in the Utah Mountains. He was a devoted husband to his wife Susie and their daughter, Jody, who was only 3 years old. In the eight months after he was infected, his weight dropped from 250 pounds to 120 pounds. He had lost all thought of his family or activity or even rational sense."

"It started slowly. First, at about three months there was memory loss and the inability to do simple math, then he developed light tremors. Eventually, these became violent seizures, accompanied by unexplainable outbursts of emotion - hysterical laughter, sometimes followed by uncontrollable crying."

"He continued to worsen and by the sixth month, he could no longer speak in sentences. Three weeks later, he stopped walking. Very quickly he lost control of his bodily functions and muscles. He was near death by the seventh month and he died a wasted, mad, drooling shadow of a man a week later."

"This is the worst thing I have seen, much worse than cancer. I wouldn't wish it on my worst enemy. The early warning signs are; insomnia, memory loss, depression, anxiety, withdrawal, fearfulness. But since these are also signs of serious physiological disorders, the correct diagnosis is frequently delayed, as if it makes any difference in the treatment of this malady."

Jack asked Dr. Whitley what the technical concept was of this disease.

The doctor answered, "It is technically a "vacuolization of neuronal cytoplasm" and it slowly affects the brain and spinal cord."

The doctor was agitated by the thought of the illness. "If this ever gets wide dispersal it will make AIDS look like a minor problem. It can be insidious and violent at the same time."

David thanked the doctor and disconnected him from the conversation. He then continued with the discussion they had been having. "The ASF scientist designed the carrier molecules into a 'binary' poison. He made it so that the 'alpha' carrier could be added to the city water system. The 'alpha' carrier is harmless by itself and could be ingested over a period of time. It is also extremely hard to detect. But, it will remain in the water for weeks and in the body for months."

Visualizing millions of people with the symptoms and disintegration the doctor had described, Jack listened in mounting distress as David spelled out the scope of the problem. "To be activated within a person's system, a second or 'beta' carrier needs to be added to the 'alpha' carrier. Once mixed, the combination becomes the poison it was designed to be. That was where the Aboud's organization inside the eOne company was critical to the ASF's plans. The second carrier would be introduced through a 'free' offering of one of the most popular bottled waters in conjunction with a major eOne water management software promotion. In this dry climate, very few if anyone at all will pass up free water."

Jack said, "Can you get some people over there to stop the distribution of the bottled water!"

David was quiet for a little bit. He sounded extremely tired and sad when he started talking again. "It's too late, eOne has been sending out free six packs of the water to every household in Tel Aviv to promote their new water management software for the last three weeks. Aboud and his goons were finished and just about to sneak home when Jacob figured out what they were doing and tried to stop them. They killed him to keep him from spoiling their getaway. By the way, you were right. They were going to kill Christi too, after they were 'done' with her."

Jack sat there for several minutes while the enormity of the problem sank in. "Can the government declare a national emergency and let everybody know what is happening. Perhaps there are many people who haven't tried the bottled water yet. They can be saved."

David sighed, "I wish it were so easy, but the leaders in both the Mossad and the government don't feel that the number of people that could be saved would be significant compared to the panic and suicide that such an announcement would generate. But that's not all."

The silence on the phone line dragged on for quite a while. Then David said with a catch in his voice, "My wife and daughter were drinking that free water this morning."

Jack said, "David, I'm so sorry." Then he thought about it and asked, "Is there no antidote that can be found in the time left?"

"Our scientists don't think so, but they will be working on it until it's too late. Perhaps your scientists in America can come up with something."

Jack said, "I will call the President immediately and get all possible resources working on it. Where are they doing this in the U.S.?"

"In the cities of; Washington, D.C., New York, Chicago, Houston, Denver, and Los Angeles."

"No!"

"Unfortunately, our agents found proof and shipping documents with the scientist in his laboratory when he was captured. They are in the same final stage that we are here. It was planned as a simultaneous strike. The last step is the 'beta' part of the poison. The last shipment of one hundred thousand cases was placed on board several ships last month on its way to the United States. There were six previous shipments."

The silence was even longer this time. Then Jack told David, "I will call you back after I talk to the President." He hung up and looked at Laura asleep in their bed. He looked over at Christi asleep on the couch and realized that the disease was at work in her as he sat there.

He stopped thinking about Christi and got down on his knees and started praying that God would intervene in the operations to poison the nations of Israel and the United States. As he prayed, the awful, dark, gut-wrenching depression that was trying to swamp him lifted when he realized that God is truly in control.

He got up and figured that it was 11:30 a.m. in Washington right then, because Tel Aviv was seven hours behind the East Coast of the United States. He probably would have a hard time getting through to the President at lunch time, so he would wait until later. Anyway, he had a local crew to get into action. Then he had another thought.

Ringing David's number again he succeeded in reaching the Mossad man. "David, did your analysts get anywhere with that sample that Christi gave you?"

David said, "No more than what we got from the scientist. Unfortunately, it is certain that her sample was some of the water with the 'beta' poison in it."

CHAPTER TWENTY-TWO

Jack continued to pray to the Lord for guidance as to what to tell the President when the time came. He stopped praying and sat quietly before the Lord. He listened for answers to the problems that were threatening the entire world.

He felt like he was half asleep and dreaming when he sensed someone approaching from a long way off. It was so very comfortable where he was, so he continued to wait and rest. The person came close to him but Jack could not see what he looked like due to the bright light backlighting him. He thought, "Lord Jesus, does this messenger claim you as his Lord?" He felt a definite positive affirmation and he sensed the overwhelming love he knew whenever he drew close to the Lord.

The "being" spoke. *"God's judgment is on your people. The idolatry and immorality of the people has raised such a stench it has reached heaven. But the Lord Yahshua's mercy abounds. Tell them that if they will turn their face to Him and repent, they will be saved. This is the time for each person to make their decision."*

Jack came to with a start. He went to the bed and woke his wife up. Sensing the urgency that showed on Jack's face she got up quickly.

Jack sat down at the small table by the window as the gray of the pre-dawn glow lightened the sky. Laura finished up in the bathroom and, wearing her robe, came over and sat down next to him. She reached out and took his hands in hers. Her hands were cold from the water she had just washed in. He looked at her small, gentle hands. He was totally choked up by his love for her and his fear that she would die from this terrible plague. He looked at her for a few minutes and then asked her to pray and ask God what He had in store for the Israeli and American people.

Laura knew Jack well enough to do it without asking why. She got down at the bedside on her knees and prayed. Ten minutes later she got up and said, "I am supposed to read Matthew 4:23 and John 3:14-17". She brought her Bible over to the table and found each chapter and verse.

"Jesus went throughout Galilee teaching in their synagogues preaching the good news of the kingdom and healing every disease and sickness among the people."

Laura then turned to the book of John.

"Just as Moses lifted up the snake in the desert, so the Son of Man must be lifted up, that everyone that believes in him may have eternal life."

"For God so loved the world that he gave his one and only Son, that whoever believes in him shall not perish but may have eternal life. For God did not send his Son into the world to condemn the world, but to save the world through him."

After she had read it she looked at Jack. "I take it we are talking about this terrorist poison, right? Jack nodded his head and Laura continued, "Well, I guess this makes it very clear that it will take real faith in Jesus to be healed from this poison. But, the majority of the afflicted people are Jewish and their faith is based strictly on the Old Testament which doesn't include Jesus. I would say that it probably isn't going to go over too well."

Jack nodded. Then he gave her the entire story. It was his nature to protect her but this time was different. He then told her about the message he had received while sitting in prayer.

Laura sat there for quite a while and thought the matter through. She wasn't the type to go to pieces or get hysterical about something that she couldn't handle. Like normal, she gave her concerns to Jesus and lifted the problem up to Him.

Jack looked out the window on predawn Tel Aviv. In the darkness, people were out and about on their business, totally unaware of the horrible disease that was already in their bodies killing them. Jack felt a great pity and sadness as he watched the doomed people plying their trades and going their way in ignorant bliss. The Bible's history contained many examples of God offering to save the Jewish people.

Unfortunately, there were that many times the people grew hardhearted and would not turn to God, thinking that their armies or science could save them. Now, it was only in the person of Jesus that the saving Balm of Gilead was being offered for the people of America and the people of Israel. How many people of the Jewish faith would turn to Jesus for healing?

He knew the same fate awaited many Americans. The unfortunate fact of life in his country was that far too many Americans lived in sin most of their lives and disregarded God. That included many church-goers who thought they were saved, even though they lived in the world six days a week and only had a passing knowledge of, or a distant faith of, who Jesus was in the world today. They didn't have an on-going loving relationship to the Son of God.

The people that did not have a relationship with the Lord, through ignorance or choice were just as doomed to hell as pagans and atheists. The proof of a person's relationship with Jesus was evident in the way they lived their lives. Many who sang the songs of praise and participated in the Lord's Supper, hurried out of church so that they could enjoy their real passions; their money, pleasure, and power. Too often, these things were seen as far more important in their normal daily lives, than God.

It was funny how the Lord had made it extremely clear, many times, to everyone, that He hated idol worship more than any other sin. He had even made that the second most important commandment. But in modern day America the majority of the people believed the marketing advertising, movies, or TV that lured them away from the one true God and seductively told them that one car, rock star, or house would set them above everyone else. Worse, yet, was the attitude that their bodies were their business and indiscriminate sex was not only just part of the game, but a requirement to be 'somebody'.

"You know, Laura" he said, "The very fact that these degenerates have poisoned a major portion of the population might wake the world up and get them to seek God."

Laura looked at Christi still peacefully sleeping after her ordeal. Laura had tears in her eyes. "It will be their choice. God is still offering to save each and every one that will turn to him. Those that don't kneel will die."

Agreeing with his wife, he kissed her on the forehead. Checking his watch he decided the time was right to call the Commander-in-Chief regardless of the business he was involved in at this time.

Picking up the phone he dialed the emergency number the President had given him, what seemed a year ago. The phone rang twice when the President himself answered. "Yes, what is it?"

Jack identified himself and asked if this was a secure phone line. The President told him to wait. A minute later he returned to the phone and said, "Jack, the line is as secure as it can be. What is the emergency?" It was obvious that this had bettered not be a social call.

Jack outlined the situation to the President and suggested his people get in touch with the Mossad for engineering and technical details. He gave the President David Zahavy's number knowing David would get the calls routed to the right person.

The President was quiet and only asked one question, "Are you sure that they are actually attacking America?"

Jack answered as best he could. "Mr. President, the information I have has come through the Mossad. Every one of them and their families are already facing death from this horrible disease. I assure you they believe that it is real and headed your way."

"I will get the ball rolling on this end. There may be a chance we can interdict some of the shipments of the second agent before it is distributed."

Jack's next comment brought the longest silence from the President. "Mr. President, I know you are a Christian and a believer so what I'm going to say will make sense to you." Jack then told him about the vision and the confirmations from the Lord and Laura.

After a long pause the President simply said, "Then there is hope after all."

Jack said goodbye and hung up. The God of the Universe was allowing the ASF to strike at the heart of the free world. And He was offering to save the world. In the meantime what was to be done about the terrorists here and there?

It was too late to go back to bed and too early to get anything done so Jack and Laura opted out to get a shower, get dressed, and go find some breakfast.

They were almost through when Laura saw Christi standing in the entry to the restaurant looking for them. She waved and the young woman came over to their table. Christi looked very serious. "We need to go over to the Mossad. A guy named David called. He said he has some new information that he needs to share with all three of us." Jack nodded and paid the bill and left with the two women. As they exited the building a Chevy Van pulled up and they recognized Sarah behind the wheel. As they walked over to the car, Mark, Craig, and Kevin came out of the hotel and headed over to them. Everyone packed into the van and headed to the Mossad headquarters building.

Reaching the garage and taking the funny elevator was old hat for half of them. The other three looked around but didn't make any comments. The soldiers preferred to take these things in stride and Christi was just impressed into silence.

David was waiting for them in the familiar conference room. He waited until everyone was introduced and seated. He looked at Jack and said, "I talked with your President this morning. He seems a very competent man." Jack thought, "Again, high praise from the Mossad."

David took a deep breath and started. "I've got to tell you that if you hadn't captured the terrorist Aboud we would not have found the scientist or known about the direness of the threat. Tel Aviv and at least six cities in America are in the same terrible shape. We share a common horror and until we find a cure we are bonded."

David sighed, "The fact that you took action while we were snarled by worrying about upsetting the apple cart is the only thing that has given us the most time to find a remedy for this thing and to deal with the terrorists before they disappear. Israel owes all of you a debt of immense proportion and we will see that debt repaid."

Jack looked up, "We were serving our own interests in rescuing Christi, and it took your help to even do that. We appreciate the honor but I think we need to get back to the U.S. and see if we can be of service there."

Jack felt a familiar urging and looked at Laura. She was staring at him and nodded her head up and down. Jack turned back to David. "David, could you and Sarah join us for a few minutes of private conversation?"

David looked up, surprised, and smiled, "A private conversation, in this building? You have to be kidding!" He laughed. "Come on tell me what you need to."

Jack mumbled, "Well, don't say I didn't try to warn you."

David furrowed his brow.

Jack looked at him for a minute. "How are you feeling since you were shot to death?"

Reflexively, David's hand went to his chest and rubbed it. "I feel fine, why?"

"Because God gave me a message this morning that he confirmed through Laura about this disease and I'm not sure how your people will take it." Jack was sure this would get everyone's attention, and it did. A silence fell over the room.

David sighed, another large sigh, and looked directly at Laura, but spoke to Jack. "If I didn't know you and your connection to God as well as I do, I would tend to dismiss this message. But since it is you and Laura, I will take it as a fact, that you have been given spiritual insight. What is the message?"

Jack felt the deep waters he was about to tread in. "God is upset with both your people and America as a people. Widespread idol worship, rampant immorality and abortions, and other sins have pushed Him to a Holy anger and He is going to let His wrath burn against the people of the Earth. God is going to allow this disease to be distributed. You know this is the truth because it already has been distributed in your country. Despite our best efforts it will be distributed throughout the United States also."

"God still loves each and every one of us. But like disobedient children, he has reached the point where he is going to let each of us follow the desires of our hearts. The difference this time will be that if a person decides not to humble themselves to God, and they've ingested the two parts of the poison, they will die, forever away from God."

David was nodding his head but he stopped when he saw Jack slowly shaking his. Jack felt real pain in his heart. "I understand what the Lord told me, and Laura confirmed it without even knowing the message I had heard." He felt the hot tears running down his face but he knew he couldn't stop. "God is willing to heal everyone that contracts this horrid disease, but this healing will only be through faith in the Messiah, his Son, Jesus."

You could have heard a pin drop the silence was so complete. Jack looked around at the assembled people and continued. "Judaism does not and has never wanted to believe that Yahshua is God's Son and the true Messiah. This is unfortunate. The Israelites in the desert, who had been bitten by a snake, could be cured simply by their belief that God could heal them when they would look upon the bronze snake that Moses held up on the standard. This time it will only be through faith in Yahshua that a person will be cured of this.

There were as many stricken looks as there were angry, hostile, unbelieving looks in the conference room. Jack added one more comment into the silence. "It's no consolation, but there are probably more hardhearted or hardheaded people in the United States that will die because they won't get on their knees, than in Israel." He stood up, dropped his headset on the table and turned to go.

One of the younger Israeli officers pointed his finger at Jack and said, "This is a bunch of garbage! God doesn't talk to people and give them messages, I should know! Your Jesus is a two-thousand year old fraud on the Jewish people! I don't believe you or your message!" He finished by spitting on the floor.

Jack was about to try and explain what he had heard when he lost control and something came out of his mouth that he hadn't planned on, and he heard that echo again. "Uri, you've tried without success for the last two years to hear from God. But God has heard every one of your prayers and wants you to open your heart and mind to Him right now."

The young man looked stunned and sat down. Everybody watched him for the next few minutes as a churning sea of emotion washed over him and registered on his face and in his posture. He fell from his seat to his knees and held his hands in the air with tears streaming down his face. Then he fell prone to the floor and spoke rapidly in Hebrew. The name Yahshua was called out several times. He then fell quiet.

Jack looked at Sarah for a translation. She shook her head and smiled. "Uri has finally heard from God. He has learned that what he thought that he "knew" all his life, was wrong, what he just said was wrong, and he asked forgiveness for his hardheadedness. The Jewish faithful still want to believe that they are still covered under God's old Covenant for salvation, but this poison is something different in that all people need to know Yahshua." She looked at Jack, "He asked Yahshua for forgiveness." The noise in the conference room swelled as people started hotly debating with each other.

Wiping his eyes with the back of his hand, Jack was glad that the Lord had used him as a spokesperson. He shook hands with David who was already on his feet looking at Uri lying on the floor of the conference room.

It was obvious that David wasn't upset or even surprised by the revelation from God. He had had his own revelation earlier.

He had never told anyone that he had met Yahshua when he died on the floor of the mini-mall. In his mind's eye he had seen Yahshua by his side. The Lord had such a look of love for David on His face that it tore at David's heart. The Lord had reached out to touch the gunshot wounds and David realized he had been completely healed. David remembered looking with wonder into the Savior's eyes and seeing love shining out like sunlight from the skies. He had never realized he had been ridden by the nameless fear of death and the afterlife all his adult life. As Yahshua hugged him he felt this fear just melt into indescribably wonderful peace.

David knew what Jack said was the truth and he was quite sure how he, and hopefully his family, were going to survive this bane on the Jewish people. He looked at Jack as he shook his hand and he leaned close to him and whispered, "Are you going to have to have God demonstrate the reality of Yahshua for each and every person in Tel Aviv?"

Jack whispered back, "No, the Holy Spirit will do the convincing. He gave David a hug and turned to leave.

Mark and Sarah walked off for a few minutes while Christi and Laura were thanking David for all his help and saying good-bye.

As the five of them got out of Sarah's van at their hotel, a group of about ten teenagers saw them and approached Christi. One guy was the spokesperson of the group. "Miss Steele? We just heard that the eOne concert is being canceled. There are a thousand Israelis that have tickets just to see you and hear you sing. If you want to go on by yourself one of our guy's dad owns a sports arena here and he said he would let us use it for a show on Saturday. Please."

He was very earnest and eager to win her over. Christi looked at Jack. Jack asked the youth, "What type of sound system does the arena have?"

Making a small frown the boy said, "Not very good for music. It's just a public address system for sports."

Jack thought for a minute and then turned to Christi. "Do you want to do a one-woman show?" She said that her band should be here somewhere and it would be great if they could put on a show after coming all the way over here and after all the grief that they've had to go through. Jack nodded, "Okay, Technology Alternatives will back your show financially. You and your guys find the sound equipment and stage and all the other stuff and I'll cover the costs and your salaries."

Sarah chimed in with, "I'll see that David gets the police to provide security and to get the proper documents and permits."

As the teenagers hurried away, another group of two young men and two young women came over and Christi shrieked, "Brad, guys, great to see you." She then introduced her four-person backup to everyone. Everyone talked at once but somehow they were able to communicate. The band got the idea about the replacement concert and wanted to talk to Christi and Jack about it.

Sarah bid everyone goodbye and took the van and headed back to the Mossad headquarters building.

CHAPTER TWENTY-THREE

As they stood there discussing what each of them were going to do, Mark suggested that Craig and Kevin provide some personal security for Christi until after her concert. They agreed but were worried about being AWOL as their leaves were officially over at midnight Sunday.

Mark said he would contact their commanders and get permission for them to remain until Christi and her band were on a plane home bound. Jack told the two soldiers that he'd make sure they were covered for travel expenses to rejoin their units after that.

They were about to break up when loud squealing tires approached them. It was the same Mossad van that the team had just gotten out of five minutes ago. The van bounced across the curb and slid to a halt between them and the street. Sarah bailed out of the passenger's side and yelled at them, "Get down, now!"

The team reacted with a speed that said volumes about their recent life-styles. Everyone, including Christi, went flat to the concrete in no time and with no regard to their clothing. The band had been touring and was a quick study. They didn't know what was going on but weren't going to debate the order.

Gunfire ripped through the air and the van sustained a heavy volume of rounds seeking anyone in the area. For unarmed civilians, it was surprising the number of guns that appeared in the team's hands from almost nowhere. Jack lunged to the safe side of the van and spotted a car with two rifles sticking out of the windows.

This being modern Israel, there were almost no civilians left in the area within seconds of the initial gunfire. Having no innocents in the way, Jack proceeded to unload all ten rounds from a Para-Ordinance P10-45 into the vehicle. His volley was matched by pistols fired by Sarah, Laura, Craig, Kevin, and

Mark. The volume of fire caused the occupants of the car to duck down, but it was a wasted effort on the terrorists' part. Another van from the Mossad headquarters building pulled alongside the car and three Uzi machine guns put holes in anything that had been missed so far, including the people in the car.

Unlike the movies, the car didn't explode. In fact it was still moving forward even though the driver was no longer in control. It came to a sudden halt when another Mossad vehicle pulled up to it nose-to-nose. Two agents got out and approached the vehicle with their Uzis at the ready. The Uzis weren't needed.

Sarah reloaded her pistol and made it disappear under her clothing. She turned to Mark and held his hand. "I heard the warning that some more of Aboud's crew were still loose and looking for you. I was coming back to warn you when I saw the car and cut off their fire lane." She looked like she was discussing a stock merger, very professional and focused.

The band had big eyes and Brad slid over by Christi. "Are we in Israel or Beirut? You seem to have some really aggressive relatives."

Christi looked at her lead guitarist and thought about her recent rescue in the eOne building. She smiled. "You haven't seen them in action at all, yet. Just be glad they are on our side!"

Mark put his arms around Sarah and gave her a passionate kiss. "Thanks. You got here right at the right time. I never even saw them. They would have had us cold if you hadn't spoiled their aim." Sarah beamed. She knew that kind of praise from Mark was hard to come by.

Laura came over and gave Sarah a hug. "You can be part of our family any time you want to. You just saved ten of us from some serious harm." She smiled and got down to business. "Now, how many more of these, 'associates' do we have to be concerned about?"

Sarah was about to answer when Mark calmly raised his H & K autoloader, leaned over Sarah's shoulder, and shot a man standing by the hotel building, aiming a handgun at them from behind Sarah. Guns started appearing everywhere again and the four band members were on the ground in a flash.

The wounded man dropped his pistol and clutched his chest. Looking at the blood on his hands he gave an intense look of hatred at the whole group. He staggered back against the wall and defiantly raised his left hand and gave Mark the finger. Another Uzi went off and bullets hit the man again. This time, he went down and stayed down.

There were suddenly dozens of police and Mossad agents everywhere. Sarah hustled the entire group into the van and drove it back to the headquarters building. While they were waiting to enter the garage, Mark yelled, "Look Out!"

While everyone was turning to see what the problem was, Mark half stood up and drove his left elbow against the large glass window in the van. Designed to pop out in emergencies, it obliged Mark and popped cleanly out of the side of the van. Mark had already drawn his H & K autoloader with his right hand and fired four rounds in rapid fire mode. He yelled, "Grenade!"

Everyone bailed out of the van and ran for the opening doors of the garage. There was a loud explosion and shrapnel pelted the bullet-holed left-hand side of the van. Jack looked back and there was a red mist spreading out about ten feet from the vehicle. Mark had obviously shot the man before he could get rid of the grenade.

Jack, Craig, Kevin, and Mark stopped and dropped to prone positions and formed a defensive line with their pistols pointing outward and firing at several people who were shooting back. Bullets were in the air again and snapping past with a crack. Jack watched helplessly as two of the attackers brought out a Soviet RPG rocket launcher and aimed it at the garage doors.

Time froze into extreme slow motion with Sarah slapping a large white button inside the garage. Laura, Christi, and the band were through the doors and running flat-out for the elevator. The four men, though, were caught outside the garage and definitely within the kill zone of the five-pound warhead on the RPG.

The terrorist launched the rocket and Jack watched as it flew toward the garage when a huge noise assaulted him from behind and drove him to the ground. A giant flare of light and fire reached outward above him, toward the rocket, which disappeared in a cloud of smoke and the debris was flung back at the launcher. Twice more the noise sounded and the two positions of the attackers disappeared as quickly as the rocket had.

Jack was having a problem hearing anything after that. But Sarah grabbed his arm and pointed at the elevator. She motioned to Mark, Craig, and Kevin.

Scrambling to their feet they ran with Sarah into the garage as the doors rolled closed. Everyone packed into the elevator and sagged against each other or a wall, whichever was handier. Brad was rather pale but tapped Christi on the shoulder. "Is there extra "hazardous duty" pay for musicians in these combat circumstances?"

In the relative quietness of the elevator Jack was beginning to get his hearing back.

The elevator came to a rest and the door opened up. The entire crew headed for the conference room but got rerouted to a private room against one wall of the open area near the cafeteria.

After checking each other to see if anyone was leaking blood they settled down onto much more comfortable couches and chairs than they would of had in the conference room. The band settled down in a corner as far away from the team as possible. Jack looked at Sarah, "What the heck was that, that, thing?"

Mark spoke up, "Planax fire."

Sarah nodded her head. "Yeah, we borrowed the idea from your anti-missile defense of your sea ships."

Jack looked a bit puzzled, "Planax fire?"

Mark smiled and nodded at Sarah, "Cute, I like it." Turning to Jack he said, "Computer-guided, depleted-uranium core bullets fired at a phenomenal rate to knock down incoming Exocet ship killers. We have them with every fleet ship to prevent a single plane or even a ground station from taking out a major ship with one missile flying close to the sea." He smiled at Sarah. "It seems that the Israelis have adapted the concept for street warfare."

She smiled, "We know the penchant for using RPGs to get into our buildings. I just never thought we would need it to defend people in the doorway." She frowned. "I also didn't know that it could automatically take out the people firing the missile."

Mark said, "It wasn't on automatic after the initial shot at the RPG. It also took out the other group that didn't fire the rocket. Someone took over control and used it to good effect."

Laura hadn't said anything for a few minutes but was getting positively irritated. "HEY! Let's get back to the original question. How many more of these low lives are there out there trying to kill us? I am getting fed up with being a target for everyone with a grudge!"

Mark looked at her, "Wait till we find out a number and then we will go hunting." He was dead serious with the emphasis on 'dead'. Everyone suddenly fell to the task of reloading their weapons and looking to Sarah for more ammunition.

Craig frowned at the pistol in his hand and he looked at Mark, "I really hadn't planned on all-out warfare or I would have brought more firepower."

At that point David walked into the room and answered Craig. "You shouldn't need it but if you do we will see that you get it." He turned to address the entire group when he spotted the four band members. "Who are they?"

Christi and Sarah explained and David rolled his eyes upward. He then summoned an aide and the band was escorted to the cafeteria for the duration. Then he continued, "It seems, I am always apologizing to you for not defending you from some kind of armed assault within our borders. So, yet again, let me extend our apologies. Despite the fact that as a nation, Israel is probably already poisoned, and putting scatology aside, we should have better control of our streets. That is being seen to, right now. I am still amazed at the ability you people have to attract trouble and then to deal with it. Most people would have left long ago or been dead."

Christi said, "Thanks, I think."

Mark asked David, "Okay, we've had fun today, what's the score? Do you have any idea of what we are up against? And, while you're at it, why are these characters so interested in killing us?"

David sat down. "I can answer some of your questions but not all. It seems that..." About that time one of the doors to the room was shoved open quickly.

The waiter was partway into the room when he realized he was staring down the barrels of at least seven handguns. Blanching somewhat, he asked in a rather high voice, "Is this a bad time? I can come back later with your food."

David shook his head as everyone put their guns away, "Sorry, recent events have made us a little jumpy."

After the waiter left the food and disappeared (unwilling to return) David continued. "As I was saying, it seems that you five have managed to capture or kill at least one member of every ASF terrorist family in Israel. So, they have declared 'Jihad' or 'holy war' on your team in revenge for the dozen or so you 'arrested' in the eOne building."

Mark looked at Sarah but addressed David, "How do they know it was us? Everyone in that group was dead or turned over to you."

David shook his head. "Apparently, there was another terrorist that somehow escaped both your attack and our sweep of the building right afterward. I would guess it was Amjad Kumate. He is slippery enough to manage that feat."

Jack was concerned. "How are we going to stop these attacks?"

Sarah said, "Easy, the Mossad will just catch or kill all of them and then they will leave you alone. This embarrassment has become a matter of honor for us."

Jack said, "Well, it looks like we need to stay here and help you, because the five of us won't do a whole lot in the States right now, but it looks like you could use some bait."

In a bizarre move, everyone on the team stood up and pointed at each other.

David laughed and threw his hands up in the air. "Here I was worried you would want to disappear back to America. NO, you want to go after terrorists. What am I going to do with you? Where were people like you while I was in America?"

Mark smiled, "You just didn't look in the right places." Pointing at Craig and Kevin he turned to Jack, "Do you think you can get the President to assign these two soldiers to us for the duration?"

Jack just nodded.

CHAPTER TWENTY-FOUR

After the Malones, Christi, and Mark left, taking the band members with them, Sarah came over to David and asked if he wanted to go out to get some different lunch than the cafeteria offered. David understood the unstated request for privacy and agreed.

The conversation revolved around regular work problems and solutions until they had left the vehicle at a mini-mall and had walked into the restaurant. After they were seated David looked at Sarah and smiled. "What is it that is so important that the company doesn't need to know about it?"

Sarah played with her salad while she made up her mind. "David, we have been friends for a long time now and even though you are my boss, I think of you as my friend and my advisor as well. I have anguished over this decision for quite a while and I'm at a point where I need your advice."

David motioned with his hand for her to continue.

Taking a deep breath Sarah looked him in the eyes and said, "I can no longer resist Yahshua and the evidence that abounds that tell me He is the true Messiah. I know that this will have me thrown out of Temple and I will become unpopular in many people's eyes, but this is much more important than any of that."

David watched her face as he asked her, "Why are you making this decision right now? Is it because of what Jack said about the only way to be healed is to turn to Yahshua?"

Sarah digested that one and came back with, "No, not really. The evidence was there for me to see in the activities of the Malones and Mark when we were working together to stop Max Lister. The coincidences that allowed us to live and totally destroyed Libya's nuclear weapons, were as graphic as the visitation on the airplane before the battle. But the thing that turned me completely into a believer of Yahshua was when He, and it was Him, saved you when you were shot. I felt His presence. I don't know how to tell you it was Yahshua rather than Yahveh, but I knew." She was emphatic on this point. She sat back and took another big breath and looked at David. "In many ways, David, I have loved you. Not a physical love but a soul to soul love. It really was destroying me when you were lying with your head in my lap and bleeding out right in front of me and there was nothing I could do." Her tears were running down her face.

David just watched her as she worked her way around to the rationale for her decision.

"I was torn in half with you dying in my arms." She continued. "Then Laura, or whoever it was speaking through Laura, told me to put aside my preconceptions and pray that God would heal you. I cannot think of a time I was more "into" a prayer in my entire life. I didn't want to lose you!"

Watching Sarah with tears in her eyes David felt the emotions of that incident pour over him. He had to take several deep breaths to keep from joining her.

Sarah stopped to take a drink of water and wipe her eyes. "While I was praying I felt this tremendous power, it was like a heat, go through me and out my hands into you. I know that was the anointing of God and at that point I felt a presence and I recognized Him. I can't tell you how, I just did. He gave me a tremendous feeling of hope and great peace. It was Yahshua there in response to that prayer. David, it was Yahshua māshīaḥ who saved you." She had reached across the table and fiercely gripped his hands in an effort to reinforce her statements so that he might understand the importance of what she was saying. She didn't want to lose him again, this time to hard-headedness and a witch's brew of hatred from Israel's sworn enemies. She knew he was prone to hard-headedness at times, frequently in fact.

David gently pulled his hands away and waved off the waiter. "Sarah, what you are doing is a big step and you really need to be absolutely sure it is the right one. Are you sure that you want to walk away from everything you've known, the faith of your people, Temple, and give your life to Yahshua and all that entails?"

Sarah smiled a tiny smile and didn't hesitate. "Yes, I'm sure. In fact, I did that when He healed you. I wanted to live for the God that was willing to extend the effort, no, a miracle to save you because the three of us were pleading with him in prayer. I was suddenly filled with such peace, love, and power, it was like I never known it could be." She looked at him with tenderness. "David, I know it is a big step. But, it is one I am praying you will make, too."

David sat back and said, "Oy! A Christian only a little while and already you're trying to convert me."

She looked at him seriously, "No, not convert, I am trying to tell you the truth, the good news of Yahshua. It's for your benefit, not mine. Please consider what I'm saying."

David laughed and laughed. Finally settling down, he reached out and took her hand. "Dearest Sarah, I know how you feel and I am proud to be your friend and sometimes your advisor, but you cannot make me love Yahshua."

She looked saddened.

He continued, "Because I already love Him and gave my life to Him."

That caused her sit up straight and stare open-mouthed at him.

David looked around the room and no one was paying any attention to them. He leaned closer to Sarah who leaned in toward him. "I was not trying to lead you on here. I just wanted to make sure you were making this choice for the right reasons."

"You see, He was with me and touched me and I was healed. It was an event that was beyond belief. I wish you could see the love in His eyes." David got serious. "I don't know 'how' He told me but I know beyond a doubt that He has that love for each and every human being on the planet. I remember thinking, 'How can you love the people that crucified you, or the people behind this horrible poisoning? That's when I realized that His love is not returned by many people but He still loves all life and desires their love in return. Regardless of our human failings, He wants us to turn to Him and worship Him and He will forgive us. But always remember, He is also a righteous judge who will punish unrepentant sinners without mercy."

David smiled, "I also remember wanting to fall on my face before Him, but He held me up and told me I would do great things in service to Him. That was such wonderful news. I am saved and needed." David sat back and shook his head.

"I 'forgot' about all of that until I was lying in bed that night and it all came back to me at once. Tears of joy started running uncontrollably down my face as my vision of Him came again and I cried and cried. I then got out of bed and got down on my knees and thanked him and asked him to be the Lord of my life."

He made a funny face with a small frown. "I was vocal enough I woke up Ruth. To say that she was somewhat concerned about my words and the apparent insanity I was speaking would be the understatement of the century. It took me most of the night to convince her I wasn't crazy."

"She is trying to make the adjustment to my not going to Temple and instead, following Yahshua and worshiping differently than she does. She doesn't understand that I have I have been touched by God and it was Yahshua. I would like you to talk to her later about this. Not now."

David took out his wallet and handed Sarah a card. She looked at it and looked up at him with a question on her face. He pointed at the card. "Messianic Jewish Rabbi", a good man to ask questions of and to listen to attentively."

After they finished lunch and headed back to the office David told her something that had been on his heart for several days. "Sarah, I'm not sure what this means, but when I was praying, one of my prayers was for you to see the light. I didn't realize that the Holy Spirit of Yahveh had already convicted you of the reality of Yahshua. But something else happened. I saw Yahshua drape a mantle of righteousness on you and call you "Esther." I'm not sure what that means but it has seemed increasingly important that I tell you that."

Sarah sat for a while as they drove back. Her mind was working on several levels at the same time. One was automatically scanning their path of travel for dangers. One was still amazed at David. Another was trying to come to grips with what being a Messianic Jew meant. While another part of her mind listened to him and wondered herself what the 'Esther' thing meant. She would have to pray about that.

As they were riding the elevator to the headquarters building, David's cell phone rang. Stepping out of the elevator he ran to his boss' office and knocked on the door. When he was admitted he entered and quickly shut the door.

CHAPTER TWENTY-FIVE

President Andrew Bollen looked carefully at each one of the forty-two people sitting around the conference table before him. Each one reflected his or her basic position and character by returning his gaze directly, indirectly, or not at all. He noted mentally that the shiftiest looks, out of the sides of their eyes, were politicians like him. The military and his cabinet were up front and willing to take the heat. Some from Congress and even the Vice President were either avoiding his eye contact or were acting like the proposal was road kill that they really did not want to look at. They merely acknowledged it grudgingly, if at all.

He cleared his throat, "People, this is not a good-will bill we are attempting to foster on the public. This will be the most critical announcement made by government since the 1776 Congress! There can be no equivocation on this. Either we are unanimous or we don't do it. If this "is a go" I want full desire and enthusiasm from each one of you."

He wasn't getting the reaction he wanted. "Okay, let me put it another way. Twenty million lives will depend on what we do this morning. Each one of those represents an average family of four. Not counting sympathy votes and other relatives, you are talking about a career maker or breaker with this decision. For all of us! I don't want lukewarm support or criticisms. I want full backing or no backing. Am I clear on this?" Every head nodded or voiced agreement with the importance of the decision.

Lance Davenport, the Senior Senator from Texas asked, "What is the predicted death toll if we do it either way?"

President Bollen looked at his Army General from the Joint Chiefs Staff. The JCS General stood up and read from a report. "Our estimate, if no word is given, is between ten and sixteen million dead, with a top possibility of twenty million. If we announce and mobilize, we could cut that number by possibly six to eight million. That depends on our interdiction efforts and if the scientists find a cure or antidote for this thing." He turned to the President, "No irreverence meant Sir, but I for one don't want to have to count on God curing me of this disease." He sat down and continued to stare at his Commander in Chief.

"That's your choice, General." The President spoke softly. "Actually, it is the choice of each person contaminated with the poison. All right! I want a show of hands. Do we alert the public to the danger and enlist their help in preventing as many contaminations as possible?" He watched with satisfaction as all hands went up immediately. "Okay, now item two. "Do we also enlist the public's assistance in finding the terrorists involved?"

The Senator from California stood up to speak. "Mr. President, colleagues, friends, let us be perfectly clear on this. We have got to have a picture of each terrorist and a name to go along with it. Otherwise every innocent Arab-American and their families are going to be hanging from trees all across this great land." He sat down.

The President stood up. "Senator Higgons is right. We don't want to have a lynch mob mentality without a target." He turned to two of the men at the table. "As Directors of the FBI and the CIA, I want a photo and a comprehensive, and terse, description of each and every terrorist involved, and their location ready to go on the air in one hour. Understand?" Both men nodded and got up from their chairs and left the room.

As the two men walked down the hallway from the White House conference room, the Director of the FBI whispered to the Director of the CIA. "How do we determine which suspects we have in the U.S. and Canada are the ones to publicize? I mean, we don't have any good Intel on which ones are involved directly in this act."

The CIA man looked at the FBI Director. "Easy, post every one of them and let God decide which ASF suspect is not going to get 'caught'. He was surprised the FBI wouldn't have thought of that on their own.

The FBI man frowned, "Carl, there are literally a dozen ASF people in Canada and at least thirty suspects in the U.S. and Mexico. It will be a blood bath once the President shows these pictures on the air!"

Carl Simmons grimaced, "Yeah, I know, but we have..." He checked his watch. "...fifty-six minutes either to play god ourselves and determine which ones are involved and possibly let the actual suspects go free, or to put them all up. I won't risk the terrorists involved in this getting away to protect the terrorist that might not be involved. Anyway, my family is probably contaminated right now with this crap and I don't really care which of the ASF killers catch hell. Their avowed purpose is to destroy Israel and the United States. As far as I can tell, there are no non-combatants." He shook hands with the FBI director as they reached their cars. "Look at it this way. Not one of the ASF is innocent because they were warned before this started of how devastating it was. My contacts were at several of their Mosque's when the general population of the ASF voted to approve the "Great Strike against the Infidels." Even if they didn't have the details they knew the death toll would be in the millions. That sounds like a declaration of war to me."

The FBI Director frowned. "Why didn't your organization warn us?"

The CIA Director gave a large sigh. "Bill, they have many of these votes and promise great destruction on the countries of Israel and the United States every year." He looked upward in regret. "We just never thought they would be able to pull one off." He got into his car and left the portico of the West Wing of the White House.

The FBI Director got into his car and thought about the hell this group was leveling on the people of the country he loved. "So be it." He thought.

In Israel David called for attention of the analysis and counter-terrorism groups, knocking on the table to get everyone's attention.

David motioned them to be quiet. "The Prime Minister has informed us that the President of the United States is going to go public with the poison story. That means that we need to do the same on the seven p.m. newscasts. We are going to coordinate with the Americans in combating both the poison and the terrorists. Our role will be to identify and locate every member of the ASF within the borders of Israel and arrest them. They are to be deported to the United States. We are also to coordinate with the CIA in pinpointing the members of the ASF, regardless what country they are in. Let's get moving people. We have less than an hour before the broadcasts."

One of the counter-terrorism team leaders stood up and asked David a pressing question. "Why are we to deport this slime to the Americans? They are not as tough on terrorists as we are."

David glanced at the assembled team leaders. "This time we don't hold a candle to what the U.S. is going to do. You'll understand better after we hear President Bollen's address in an hour."

CHAPTER TWENTY-SIX

Every television station, radio station, and Cell Phone Company went with an emergency plan designed in the nineteen seventies and updated one year ago for getting the attention of as many people as possible in the United States and Canada. The only new additions were World Wide Web, Facebook, Twitter, and Blog announcing over every ISP in the country. Every person in the United States, Canada, and Mexico were told to watch television, listen to the radio or public announcement at noon, Eastern Standard Time, without fail. Their very lives depended on doing that.

This announcement had been tailored by warfare psychology scientists to command attention from the public as a prelude to nuclear war if time allowed. The effect was one of no-nonsense importance, period. Since it was recorded, there was no talking back to it and no denying it as it was repeated every five minutes until noon.

At precisely 12:00 noon, EST, the President appeared on all broadcast, cable, cell-phone, and satellite stations.

"Ladies and Gentlemen of the free world," a solidly sober President started. "I come before you today with a terrible warning and a request for help." There is a deadly attack against the population of at least six American cities going on as I speak. A terrorist group has launched biological warfare against the nations of Israel and the United States. They have developed a 'binary' poison which requires a victim to ingest both parts before it becomes activated. The first of these poison agents have been placed in the drinking water supplies of at least the cities of Washington, D.C., New York, Chicago, Houston, Denver, and Los Angeles." The President waited for a second while the public absorbed the locations

He then continued, "There are no guarantees that other cities are not also under attack at the present time. These are the six cities that have been confirmed. The second part of the poison is present in one manufacturer's bottled water." A picture of one of the bottles was shown for a few seconds on the television screen.

"If you have any bottled water with the brand name, *"Maximum Desert Ultra Clean"* that is unopened, do not, I repeat, do not open it, drink it, or throw it away. Save it for analysis. I will speak more on that in a moment."

The President came to the part that was the hardest part of the short speech. "Our scientists are working around the clock to find an antidote or cure for this poison. If there is any chance, they will find it. But, until they do, this poison is fatal and has no known cure. Once poisoned, a person will not feel anything or know that there is anything wrong for several months. Therefore, we are very hopeful that a cure can be found. Israel has developed a quick and easy saliva test to detect the disease. They have shared that with us and we are distributing the tests to every city in the U.S. and Canada. We will send tests to Mexico before the week is out. We will use these to determine if you or your loved ones may have become poisoned."

"I know it sounds unreasonable, but there is no reason to panic. We have time on our side. If you act unreasonably crazy, it will not resolve the problem and could get in the way. Here is what you are to do. There are three things I want every American, Canadian, and Mexican citizen to do starting immediately. One, search your home, your business, your vehicle for bottles of water like we showed you a moment ago. We will display it again in a few minutes. By tomorrow, there will be military collection posts throughout every city in America, and I expect in Canada and Mexico also. Take all of your unopened bottles of water to these designated collection posts. You will need to tell them when and where you found the bottle and how long it was there, if you know. I want all businesses that sell this brand to take them off the shelves and package them up for delivery to the posts. Write on them the date they were delivered to you and by whom, as well as the name of your store."

The President sat back slightly in his seat. "Two. In less than a week there will be a list of medical posts. Again, these will be military posts with civilian doctors. I urge every American to go to a post and be checked for the poison. We need to know how many people have been poisoned and where they are so that we can distribute help proportionately."

"Three. After I finish speaking there will be a presentation by the FBI with photographs of suspected terrorists. I repeat, these are only suspects and need to be questioned to determine if they are in any way connected with this heinous plot to kill our people. I want every man, woman, and child to look out for these people. There are a lot of them so you need to study them carefully. Get your recording equipment set up because they will repeat this part of the broadcast several times throughout the day."

"People, this is very important. You are not to try to apprehend these suspects yourselves. If they are not involved, then they could get hurt. If they are involved, then you could get hurt. Call your local police, the FBI, or the Army at the numbers that will be shown. I need everyone's help to find the people that are involved and to bring them to justice. This will not be tolerated and these people will not be allowed to get away with this. As your President I assure you that every aspect of law enforcement is already alerted and will comb the country to find these people. Remember, help us find them. Do not take the law into your own hands! You could be wrong and hurt or kill an innocent person and you will be prosecuted for that to the full extent of the law."

Looking into the camera the President was obviously very earnest when he made the next appeal to the public. "This nation was founded on the basis of the love of God and His Son, Jesus Christ. I know that there are many "religions" represented in this great country and they all make their claims to represent God. People, we don't have the time for a theological debate on this subject, I am a Christian, as everyone knows from the election. God has made it clear that

He is allowing this disease to attack our people because we have drifted away from His love and many are living in sin."

He pointed at the camera. "Notice that I did not say that He was causing it. We have lost His protection from this because of the sinfulness of our people. You know what I'm talking about, large scale acceptance of abortions and loose sexual immorality, homosexual acts, and lust have offended the Lord of the Universe. Don't cry foul. Your rhetoric doesn't matter anymore. God in His justice has tried to appeal to each of us. He is now letting us reap the rewards of choices not to live according to His word. But! He is offering each of us one more chance. If you will turn to Jesus and repent of your sins and take Him as the "Lord of your life", and live for Him, He will heal you of the disease. Those of us fortunate enough to not have the disease need to comprehend this clearly. If you want God's protection from these and possibly worse things, turn to Him.

The President bowed his head for a few seconds, "people of the United States." He intoned with his head down. Then he looked into the camera. "I now want to outline what we as a nation are going to do as a measured response to this evil and unwarranted attack against our country. First, I have discussed this with the Congress through their leaders and as of this minute the United States of America is at war with the organization known as the Arab Strike Force or ASF. If any country in the world wants to defend this terrorist organization, or attempts, in any way, to hamper our search for and apprehension of every person who swears allegiance to this group, then the United States of America will immediately declare war against that nation. To the nations of Syria, Lebanon, Libya, Iran, the Sudan, Zyngola, North Korea, India, Pakistan, and Afghanistan, let this broadcast back up the official notice sent to your governments in the last hour. I do not want to trample on any nation's sovereignty or their religious rights. But make no mistake about this. The United States and its allies in this cause, of which there are already over thirty at this time, will not tolerate your allowing these criminals to remain within your borders. You have forty-eight hours to locate and deport any person known to be a part of this organization. If they have nowhere to go, then give them to us."

The President stood up, causing the cameramen to scramble to focus on his face. He slammed his fist onto the desk. "If you want to side with them, then so be it. We will attempt to keep collateral damage to your civilians and non-government or non-military buildings and equipment to a minimum." Then he frowned. "But the way your governments tend to mix military and civilian operations together, and the probable use of heavy weapons including nuclear weapons, it will be very hard to prevent high levels of damage to your populations as well as your infrastructures, in those cases."

The President looked directly into the lens of the camera. "There will be no extensions, delays, or excuses. We and the Israelis know who the people in the AFS are and can match each one by a simple DNA field test. We also know where they are at present. The United States is prepared to go door-to-door if necessary, to find these people. Find them we will!"

The President clasped his fingers on the desk and leaned on them. "There will be no saber-rattling or paper-tiger garbage this time. The ASF, by its cowardly and horrific assault on our population and that of Israel, has become a direct threat to the people of our two nations and we are coming to get them right now. You have been warned."

President Bollen sat down again. The cameramen were ready this time and things went better. "We are in the process of calling up all reserve armed forces at the moment. I have instructed the Chiefs of Staff to notify all branches of the military that they are on a wartime footing as of this moment. Special groups have been tasked to identify and apprehend the members of this organization and will have the full backing of the U.S. military in all operations outside the country. Any resistance by military forces or attacks on our personnel will be construed as an act of war and will be treated as such. Therefore I have asked each of your governments to declare your intentions within the hour. If there is organized resistance on a large scale then we will use any weapons at our disposal to gain our objectives." The President looked nonchalantly at the camera. "This means if a country wants to hide and or protect the Arab Strike Force or its members, then we will view that country as an enemy, and eliminate as much of that country as necessary, to ensure the elimination of the ASF being harbored in that country.

I hope that I have made things perfectly clear to any government that wants to debate this and to the people that live in that country." He looked up at the clock on the wall behind the camera. "Your forty-eight hours started ten minutes ago. I also expect your governmental official response to be in our hands within the hour. Failure to respond will be accepted as a de facto declaration of war."

The President got up and walked away from the desk. The news conference was definitely over.

CHAPTER TWENTY-SEVEN

Five days after the President's speech, the Director of the FBI was composing a report to the President when he was interrupted by his Assistant Director Mike Stoval. Looking up from his paperwork he gave Mike a questioning look.

Mike was reading a report as he came over and sat on the corner of his boss' desk. This was something only 'Iron Mike' could get away with in the Bureau. No one else would even dare.

Mike looked up from the report. "Listen to this. Out of the thirty known operatives of the Arab Strike Force in the United States, thirty-eight have been captured. Most of them due to information received from the public. Eight have been killed in shoot-outs with our agents, police, or in two cases, that same public."

The Director shook his head, "thirty-eight out of thirty?"

Mike nodded, "Seems that there were more here than we thought. Of course that is nothing new with terrorist organizations."

"But this is the kicker. Two of the top ASF lieutenants were discovered in a traffic jam in rush hour traffic in downtown LA this afternoon. Apparently, word spread like wildfire and a crowd estimated at two to three thousand people surrounded their car and forced them to abandon the vehicle. When one of the suspects made a laughing comment that everybody there was going to die horribly the crowd 'stoned' them to death."

The Director thought about it for a few seconds and said, "How very Biblical of them."

Mike continued reading, "When the Army and LA firefighters got through the crowd they had to 'dig' the suspect's bodies out of, get this, piles consisting of pieces of pavement, curbing, bricks from the surrounding buildings, eight manikins, various street signs, a bus bench, shoes, magazines, newspapers, clothing of all kinds, several dozen canes and bicycles, two porch swings, a small Volkswagen, and, apparently, a set of dentures."

The Director sat back in his chair and said, "Oh my!"

Mike looked at the other pages of the report. "There have been thousands of reported locations called in on the remaining four terrorists whose pictures have been distributed across the country. I'm concerned that totally uninvolved Arabs such as foreign students or Arab-Americans are going to be lynched or torn to pieces if we don't tone down the hunt."

The Director nodded his head and pointed to the document on his desk. "That's just what I was telling the President."

As the extent of the horror settled in on the millions of infected people, the prevailing attitude was one of dismay, abject horror, and inevitability. People who were, or thought they were, infected became mad or suicidal. Thousands of people took their lives to prevent going through the insidious decay and loss of their identity. Thousands more tried to end it all but botched the job resulting in more human suffering and placing extreme burdens on their families and local medical community resources.

As the tests confirmed the disease in millions of Americans the cry for revenge rose on the social and political agendas such that it was consuming the politicians as much as the infected populace. People wanted to strike at anything or anybody for the evil that was overcoming them. There were riots and local fights and sometimes bloodbaths to vent their frustration and fear of the gruesome death that whole cities faced. Uninflected people learned quickly not to boast about their healthiness for fear that an angry, infected person would explode and do them harm for their audacity for not catching the illness.

In one home in Houston, the father sat unmoving in his chair with the reports in front of him that his entire family had contracted the disease. He had three little girls all less than ten years old. He couldn't bear the thought of them suffering the debilitation and loss of dignity that the disease was to cause them. They didn't hold with religion so they didn't have any hope at all. So he went to the closet and took out a chemical he had purchased last year to kill stray dogs. He mixed the poison with a "power drink" and took the drinks out to his family in the back yard. It was a typically hot day in Houston and the drinks went down quickly even though they tasted "funny." In less than fifteen minutes the whole family was dead still sitting in their chairs under the blazing sun. They were discovered by the wife's mother when she came to babysit the girls that evening. It made the news because it was an obvious statement of how most people with the disease were feeling.

The President's comments concerning God's reprieve had several notable effects. Millions of people decided that it was time that they should take Jesus as their Savior. Many others seeing a conspiracy in the disease and announcement, denounced Christianity as the cause for the whole thing and burned churches and hounded well-known Christians as the instigators of the disease. Several "religions" went on the air denouncing the President and stating flatly that Jesus Christ could do nothing to save a person. The New Age gurus argued that the disease could not kill you if you (as god) told it not to. The Christian Scientists agreed with the New Agers.

Overseas the operations were receiving more cooperation than at home. Countries that had always defended the rights of terrorists groups to operate out of their borders had been assured by Russia, China, and Germany that the United States was not bluffing on this one. The choice was clear, the actions immediate. Anyone in the ASF was arrested and placed in the hands of the U.S. military for transportation to the United States. Resistance was not tolerated, and for every terrorist that demanded anything but surrender their bodies were turned over to the U.S.

Field DNA tests were run to ensure that every known member of the AFS was accounted for. Since there were less than five hundred known ASF members worldwide and the U.S. was promising to destroy hundreds of thousands if not millions of people for non-cooperation, the choice was simple. Self-preservation was much more important than political ideals at this point.

Human nature being what it is, there was an exception. The small newly-formed country of Bagistan, with a population of eight thousand, decided to stand up to the U.S. threats. They only had eighteen of the AFS within their country but decided not to cooperate. The President ordered the First and Second Calvary into Bagistan to locate and secure the terrorists.

Before the U.S. military reached the border, a coalition of Arab states had massively invaded the tiny country and delivered the twelve surviving terrorists and the bodies of the dead terrorists to the U.S. forces. Bagistan no longer existed as a nation. The remaining fifty-five hundred citizens, mostly women and children were absorbed into the neighboring countries and the rubble of Bagistan's only city was left as a monument covering the bodies of their small army as a warning. The major Arab nations wanted to convince the western world that they had nothing to do with the ASF and that meant the entire Arab world whether they agreed or not.

The United Nations went ballistic. The General Assembly condemned the United States for the extermination of Bagistan and for forcing the world to surrender the entire Arab Strike Force. The body of the UN wanted the U.S. and Israel to free the 'revolutionaries' immediately and pay reparations to them.

As directed by the President and the Congress, the United States Ambassador to the UN informed the entire United Nations that they were no longer welcome as an organization in the United States of America and were, in fact, bordering on declaring their organization at war with the United States. They had one week to move their operations out of the US. After that, all visas would be revoked and the non-U.S. UN personnel would be considered illegally in the country. All ambassadors and representatives of sovereign countries were, of course, welcomed to apply for their own national and personal visas.

The United States, followed immediately by Britain, Canada, Israel, and the European Union, withdrew their military and financial support of the organization and it collapsed completely in two days. The small nations that had used the UN to demand equal footing with the large countries and other selected causes, had to try to sell their complaints, demands, and objections one-on-one to any nation that would listen. Most did not want to listen.

CHAPTER TWENTY-EIGHT

David sat back in his office chair and pinched his nose and pressed against his eyes to relieve the strain of the last two days. Since the announcements of the American and Israeli governments, the panic had come and gone and the public was cooperating. The report he had just reviewed made a horrifying summation of the situation.

Of the 346,542 Jewish residents of Tel Aviv/Jaffa, over 80 percent had tested positive for the poison in its active form. The ironic part was that over 84,000 Arab residents of the cities had also tested positive. That was over 92 percent for them. Altogether there were 362,000 citizens poisoned with no cure in sight.

David sighed deeply. He had been following the religious clamor and temple prayers and pleas to God for salvation and elimination of this disease. The results were the same afterward and he knew that the majority of the people of Tel Aviv and Jaffa were not going to embrace Yahshua even if it meant that they would die. He recalled Yahveh calling the Jewish people "a stiff necked people" and had to agree with that summation.

There was a knock at his door and Sarah opened the door at his response. He showed her the figures and watched her concern wash across her face. She put the report down and sat down. "Mark just told me the latest count of the poisoned people in America is over eighteen million."

They just sat there and thought about the deaths of all the people in their two countries and the ramifications such mass death would have in the future.

Sarah turned her head and looked at her good friend. "David, I have been praying about your comment that Yahshua put a mantle on me and called me 'Esther'. I think I know what it is I am supposed to do."

David looked at her for a few seconds. "Did you speak to the rabbi whose card I gave you?"

Sarah nodded her head. "Yes I did." Her dark eyes flashed and she took on a serious attitude. "I think I am to lead a nationwide prayer session of the Messianic Jewish faithful and ask Yahshua to forgive all his children and heal them."

David's eyes widened. "That's quite a step for a brand-new Christian isn't it?"

"I'm not sure it matters how long I have been a Christian in name. The Lord wants me to organize a three day fast culminated by a televised call to prayer. I am supposed to lead a prayer of repentance and supplication to Yahveh, God of the Universe, for healing. The Messianic community is not only behind me, they have received the same leading and in their prayers I was pointed out. Go figure. Yahveh surely does move in strange ways."

David sat up and fixed her with a glance. "What makes you think any of the Israeli television stations are going to televise your prayer session? They are pretty much Jewish-oriented and don't give the Messianic movement very good coverage."

Sarah clenched her fists and slammed them down on the table surface. "They just have to! This is too important for the entire nation of Israel! Do you realize that the Messianic Jewish population is completely free of the disease?"

David nodded. "As am I, well, we will see. Of course you realize that this is a 'fleece' of sorts?"

She asked, "How can this be a fleece?"

"Well, if this is something Yahveh wants done, then the stations will give you coverage. If they don't then maybe it isn't Yahveh."

Sarah nodded her head up and down. "Good point. I like it. Self-confirming and self-reassuring. I for one will believe in the Lord and his leading. I expect that the TV coverage will be there on Saturday. The fast starts at sun-down today with the last day being the Thursday before the Sabbath. The prayer session is immediately after Shabbat on Friday evening at seven p.m."

David smiled. "How interesting that it coincides with the Sabbath. Well, I for one will be fasting and praying that the Lord will heal stiff necked Jews like my wife and my children."

Sarah could only nod and try to realize the pain he felt.

CHAPTER TWENTY-NINE

Jack showed the test results to Laura. None of their team had the disease including Christi. Quietly sending a prayer of thankfulness to Jesus Jack filed the report in his briefcase. "Did you hear that Sarah will be fasting, starting tonight, through Thursday with the Sabbath directly leading into a nationwide prayer by the Messianic population of Tel Aviv to heal the infected?"

Laura said, "Yes I did. I agree with her that this is a leading from the Lord and a petition to His Father that needs to be done. I understand all of the media outlets including broadcast TV is going to cover her prayer session."

Jack laughed. "But the question is, are they covering it to see it fail or to see it succeed?"

"It doesn't matter which reason they are doing it for, it will succeed and God will be glorified, which is what He wants, so that people will question and seek and turn to Him." Laura bowed her head for a minute and asked Jack, "Are you fasting too?"

Jack looked introspective for a few minutes and nodded his head. "Oh yeah. I'm fasting and praying with Sarah. I take it that you and Christi are too, right?"

Laura nodded her head. "I want to do my part to seek God's forgiveness for all the infected people in both countries. I love you, Jack."

That caught him off balance and he reached out and gently pulled his wife into his embrace. "I love you too, sweetheart. I feel that there are vast forces moving just out of sight right now and we are standing on the brink of a bottomless chasm. I remember feeling like this the first time when I accepted the locker key in the men's store in Denver."

They sat there hugging each other for a long time. Eventually the phone rang and Jack answered it.

The man's voice on the phone asked if he was Jack Malone. When he said he was the man asked if he and his wife could meet with Jack and Laura that afternoon. They had been sent by the Christian community in Greece with information concerning the ASF and that they had been given Jack's name by the Lord during prayer. Jack asked for their names, telephone number, and what hotel they were at and said he would be in touch.

Calling David he passed on their names and the message in the event it was a ruse by the ASF to catch them unaware.

David said he'd check them out and call Jack back as quickly as possible.

As they waited they went over their plans to head back to the U.S. the next day.

David's call indicated that the couple seemed to be who they said they were. He said that they were members of the Greek Christian Church and had arrived that day from Greece and matched their photos. He suggested that Jack pick up a microphone/camera from the headquarters before the meeting in the event there was more to the meeting than they expected.

Jack returned the call and spoke to Derrick Carmelos. They agreed to meet in an hour in the restaurant in Derrick's hotel.

Jack and Laura walked into the restaurant a few minutes early and took a table. When Derrick and his wife Katherine walked in and came to the table, Jack had an unexpected reaction. Derrick was a fit young man in his middle twenties with the physique of an athlete in top form. He had a full head of dark black hair and a face that was almost classically beautiful with full lips and a roman nose. He also had dark eyes with full lashes. That was all well and good but his wife was shockingly beautiful. Laura paled next to her. She also had fit body but with generous curves and a graceful neck. Her face was framed with long auburn hair and a mouth that looked too good to eat honey. Every hormone in Jack's body stood up and tried to get to the side of his body closest to her.

They shook hands and sat down. Somehow, Jack sat next to Katherine and Laura was sitting next to Derrick. The small talk slid by without Jack remembering any of it. He was consumed with the sight and perfume of the dark-headed woman. Her voice was so incredible he wondered how it could be so seductive and yet so innocent at the same time. He drank in the vision and totally ignored the other two people at the table.

When she was explaining the message they had been given she reached out and placed her hand on Jack's. It was like a voltage passed through his hand and arm and warmed his heart.

Somewhere deep in his mind alarm bells started to sound. But it was such a little sound compared to the way he was feeling at the moment. Then he thought for a second. How was he feeling? Randy as a goat in heat. He was having such lustful thoughts and desires that it jarred him. He glanced at Laura and was surprised to see her staring at Derrick like a love-struck teenager. A piano began to play and people got up to dance on the small dance floor near the piano bar. Derrick tipped his head and Laura got up and walked over to the floor and began to dance with the man.

While he was watching his wife he felt Katherine snuggle up next to him. Talk about your desire and urges. Jack lost all thought about Laura at that contact and turned to Katherine only to find her about two inches from his face, with a rapturous look on her face as she pressed up against him and leaned into him for a kiss.

One word forced its way through the desire and flared before Jack's eyes, SIN! It made Jack pull away from the woman against his own desire. He needed to get some thinking room. Somewhere this woman wasn't. He tried to smile and failed. "I really need to go to the men's room. Hold that thought until I get back."

Not giving her a chance to dissuade him, Jack unwrapped himself from her arms and rose. He turned and almost ran to the bathroom. He was literally consumed with desire to ravish this unknown woman. He locked himself in a booth and closed his eyes. Her image was there, too. He prayed to Jesus to help him overcome this obsession. Her effect began to disappear and lose its hold on him so he could think clearly. He had an idea what was going on and realized he was jeopardizing Laura by being away from her. He charged out of the bathroom and spotted his wife in the embrace of the Greek man.

A white heat flashed through his body cleansing all testosterone and interest in Katherine. He walked over to Derrick and clasped his shoulder in a hold he practiced frequently in the Dojo. The nerve grouping there was sensitive to pressure placed just so. Derrick's left arm fell from around Laura like it was lifeless and he turned to face Jack. Laura was speechless and looking from one man to the other to figure out what the problem was.

Jack expected the other man to become angry, but he didn't. He massaged his shoulder and smiled at Jack. "Didn't you like my wife?" the question was asked with such innocence it almost threw Jack off.

Jack smiled at Derrick, "She's very nice but we have to be going. I will call you tomorrow and we can continue this conversation." With that he pulled Laura to the table and got her purse. He smiled at Katherine, "Sorry, but we have to run." He then led Laura out of the restaurant and to their car.

As they reached the car he saw Laura looking at him. "What?" He asked.

She quietly said, "Jack, you're breaking my hand."

Jack let go and realized he had been holding on way too tight. "Sorry, get in the car, please."

Laura got in and waited while Jack backed out and then he stopped. He reached over and took her purse. He dumped the contents into her lap. She didn't say anything. Jack leaned over and whispered in her ear, "Is there anything in there that isn't yours?"

Laura seemed confused and upset by the question but looked through the items in her lap. She noticed a compact that wasn't hers. Startled, she looked at Jack and nodded, pointing at the compact.

Jack picked up the compact and exited the car. He found a truck with the windows open and placed the compact on the truck seat. He then got back in and drove them back to their hotel. Laura was quiet the whole way.

When they were in their room she turned on him furiously and asked, "What is the matter with you? I know we've been a little busy trying to stay alive the last few months but I was enjoying dancing!"

Jack nodded, "I'm sure you were but I needed to interrupt you because I thought you were in danger."

Laura laughed, "From whom? Derrick and his wife? They aren't the enemy. They were nice people and I was enjoying their company."

Now Jack wasn't sure that he had done the right thing. "Honey, I'm sorry if I spoiled a good time but I'm afraid that there was more going on there than friendship." In his mind he asked the Lord to cleanse his wife's mind of any demonic influences.

He then told her that he loved her and that there was no other woman in the world that meant anything to him than her. For the first time that didn't seem to move her. Pressing on, he then explained in detail his immediate desire to spend the rest of his life with Katherine and completely forget about her.

He let that sink in for a few seconds and then reminded her of something. "One reason you say you love me is because I analyze everything and look at it from every angle if I have time, right?"

She nodded. Jack continued. "I'll tell you one thing. This experience of total lust was so unnatural for me it jarred me into thinking that something was wrong."

Laura stared at nothing for a long time and Jack started to wonder if he had really hurt their relationship.

Then Laura turned to him and said, "Jack, I am so sorry. I completely understand your reaction to Katherine, because I had exactly the same unnatural reaction to Derrick. I wanted him to love me and do things to me I don't even think about normally. I don't understand how I could suddenly be so drawn to someone, so consumed with lust that I would completely forget about you."

Jack nodded in agreement, "The operative word here is 'unnatural'! I'm just like any other man and will get interested in a pretty woman, but I can control those 'old man' urges. The new man I became in Christ sees behind the lure and urge. But this was so completely overwhelming I just… I just lost it."

Laura came over and sat down by Jack and put her fingers over his mouth. "Don't explain any more. I am pretty aware of how guys are 'turned on' and I know that those things don't normally affect a female. But for me, this was way beyond simple lust or puppy love. He completely captivated me and I would not have cared whatever he did as long as I could be with him. Now it makes me sick and angry at the same time. How dare he do this?"

Jack got up and went over to the phone. It was about eight in the evening in Tel Aviv which would make it around eleven in the morning in Denver. He placed the call and when he got an answer, he asked for Alan Throman.

When the older man answered the phone, Jack greeted him and asked how he was doing and if the church was completely over their baptism. Alan Throman laughed and said, "Better than ever, that goes for both the church and me. But this is more than just a social call, isn't it?"

Jack agreed with him, "Yes, it is, but I have been praying that everything was all right with you. You were there for us at a critical time and I want to be there for you, too." Then Jack explained briefly where they were and what had brought them to this point, including the Carmelos and the events of the evening.

The Minister was quiet for a while and then said, "I have an idea what is going on and you are correct in thinking this 'attraction' of you and your wife is 'unnatural'. I think you are being besieged by a pair of demons, probably demons of lust. But I have a friend who is an expert in this field. He roams all over the globe performing deliverance for people that need his help. As the Lord would have it, I think he is near your location right now. His name is Gary Eisenthal. I advise you to wait until you've talked to him before you meet the Carmelos again."

Jack agreed and gave the Minister his hotel name and address and his phone number and promised to keep in touch and let him know what was going on.

CHAPTER THIRTY

Gary Eisenthal was near all right. He was in Jerusalem and drove to Tel Aviv that evening.

Jack opened the door to their room and admitted the thin man. He had a quickly fading hairline of light brown hair and a mustache of the same color. The rest of the man including his clothes was nondescript. The only feature that one noticed immediately was his eyes. He had a flame of intensity and intelligence that would have looked fanatical on a less self-affecting person. After Jack introduced him to Laura, Gary explained his ministry.

He accepted a cup of tea from Laura. He collected his thoughts and began to talk. "I have been given a position as a spiritual warrior for the Lord Yahshua. The scriptural authority is from the scriptures in Luke 9:1 *"When* Yahshua *had called the Twelve together, he gave them power and authority to drive out all demons and to cure diseases."* Also, in John 14:12 Yahshua said, *"[12] I tell you the truth, anyone who has faith in me will do what I have been doing. He will do even greater things than these, because I am going to the Father."* So while I was praying that I wanted to serve Yahveh, the Holy Spirit 'graced' me with spiritual discernment and a heart for deliverance. I have been in the trenches ever since. Have either of you ever seen a demon, or for that matter, an angel?"

Jack recounted the original battle between the demon and Yahshua in the basement in Colorado and the visions that he had seen in Houston and on the plane when they were after Max Lister. Laura told him about her dreams. He nodded, "Dreams and visions are one of God's ways of communicating with you when He feels it is necessary. I believe during the combat, what you witnessed was a momentary discernment. Spiritual discernment is one of the gifts of the Holy Spirit. It allows a person to determine, and quite frequently, see the spiritual forces on both sides. Sometimes, during deliverance, I have spoken to demonic forces and occasionally I am allowed to see the actual demons afflicting the people I work with. Once I was privileged to see two large angels contain an evil spirit that was trying to attack me."

Laura furrowed her brow, "Are you talking about exorcism?"

Gary chuckled, "That name carries way too much in the way of images and is basically misleading. I prefer the name 'deliverance' because what we do is pray a prayer of deliverance using the power and authority of Yahshua that is within the believer. We try to 'deliver' unwilling captives away from the demonic and into freedom. Now, before we discuss your particular case we need to be sure of your 'spiritual health'. If what Alan told me is correct, then you both are in considerable danger, if you're not as bullet-proof as you can be."

Jack frowned, "Bullet-proof?"

Eisenthal smiled, "Relax, everyone is subject to spiritual forces. The less you know about them the more they can run your life without your even suspecting anything. You know that as a Christian your spirit belongs to Christ and no one can take you away from him, right?" When they nodded he went on. "That's okay as far as the basics go. A Christian believer cannot be 'possessed'. That means Satan can't 'possess' your spirit, but that doesn't mean he doesn't have a legal right to oppress your life in a heavy duty manner. Demons can make your life a living hell right here on Earth or they can try to woo you into Satan's camp and away from God."

Gary took a drink of his tea. "When you became a Christian, and Alan told me that was pretty dramatic, you took on the new spirit that the Holy Spirit gives you when he comes to live in you. Unfortunately, the old man is there in you too. You ask God to help you live right and resist temptation, but there is always those 'urges'. For some it's the urge to cheat, others it's the urge to go astray or lie constantly. It is different for each person depending upon their background before they gave their life to Yahshua.

He got up and paced slowly back and forth. "One way to understand is the concept of 'doors'. If you give in to an urge and slip into, say, immoral activities like unfaithfulness or pornography obsession, then you have opened up a door of 'legality' for a demon."

Laura looked at Jack and asked, "How do you mean legality?"

Gary looked at her for a few seconds and his eyes seemed to burn right through her. "Read Job and you'll see what I mean. There are spiritual laws in the spiritual world and the demons have to respect them. True, their job is to murder, steal, and destroy, but they have to follow the rules or they cannot function. Regardless of their enmity toward God, Satan and the demons get their power from God like everything else in this universe. Their desire to attack a believer cannot be acted upon until they get permission to by a sinful action on that Christian's part or God allows it, as in the case of Job. This is why it is so important to avoid sin in every case if you can."

He sat down again and spoke with some intensity. "You can ask forgiveness for a sinful action and God in His mercy will forgive you. But, sins have consequences here on earth because they were committed. You may have opened a door that will allow a demon to affect you. He now has the right because of the sinful action. Let me give you an example. Let's say a married woman has an affair because she is bored at home and seeks some excitement. Sex outside of marriage is sinful. Her husband, if he finds out, can forgive her and God will forgive her if she truly repents and asks for His forgiveness. But, the man she slept with may not be a believer, in fact probably is not, and he could have demonic activity in his life. By agreeing to go against God's wishes, she has given an open door to his demons to work in her life. Not only that but any demons he has acquired from other partners. These are called 'soul ties' and can be very hard to root out. Think of them like a spiritual AIDS that can transfer to many people. They are controlled primarily by sexual demons but can include demons of death or other demons like depression."

Jack thought about Gary's information. "Is that the extent of the problem?"

Gary laughed, "If it only were. There are also generational demons, ones that are from unrepentant sin from your ancestors, territorial demons, and many more." He noticed the distressed look on both of the Malone's faces. "Don't give up. God is much bigger than all of the demons and will keep you free of their clutches if you ask Him to. If you will truly repent of your sins, and if you ask Him, God will tell you what they are, and walk holy before Him, the demons and other unholy things cannot stay in the light of the Holy Spirit that is in you when you walk holy before your Lord God."

A question that had been bothering her so Laura asked Gary, "Gary why should we use the name Yahshua instead of Jesus?"

Gary smiled in return. "Because Yahshua is the true name of the Messiah, the Christ that came to Earth to save Yahveh's people."

Jack frowned, "Is it that critical? I mean, isn't God big enough to handle the use of the name Jesus?"

Gary decided to give them the condensed version of the true name of the Lord of the Universe. "First, understand that the Old Testament Hebrews felt it was a grave sin to pronounce the sacred name of God, which was only pronounced using the four letters YHVH, which, inspired by God's Holy Spirit, appear in the Old Testament over 6,800 times. It is pronounced Yahveh."

"English translators on their own volition replaced God's name with something entirely different. They took away and added to God's Word by replacing His personal name Yahveh with the capital letters LORD and GOD or with the Hebrew hybrid word Jehovah.

In perverting the text, the English translators actually broke the Third Commandment since they made the name vain, that is, of no effect

Gary strode back and forth across the room as he put forth the arguments for correctly naming God and His Son. "Consequently, we have been charged to remember, to commemorate and to memorialize God's sacred name. Yet, most modern translators have done just the opposite and have nearly wiped God's sacred name from the memory of His people."

Gary sat on one of the beds and continued. "One thing most Christians are ignorant of is that the Name of the True God appears within the name of the messiah. The son of Mary was not Jesus but Yahshua. Jesus is a Greek word. The letter "J" doesn't even exist in Hebrew. In fact, the letter "J" wasn't even devised until the fifteenth century. The Greeks looked at Yahshua and were stumped because Greek does not have a YAH or a SHU sound. So the Greek translators transliterated the name into a derivation of their god's name which was Zeus and called Him Ya-Zeus because a lot of Zeus worshippers, such as Constantine, felt the merge of names would honor their newly adopted Lord. Ye-Zeus was then corrupted further into Jesus." Gary threw up his hands in irritation.

Then he continued, "Yet the angel Gabriel told Mary that the Messiah's Name, which was given by Almighty God Himself, was of special significance. It is of great importance when you pray to the Lord, especially in times of spiritual warfare, when you call on the Name of the Lord it has a precise meaning of prophetic importance. Gabriel said that He would receive this Name because "He shall save His people from their sins."

Gary got up and started pacing again. "Every Hebrew scholar will tell you that the Name given through Gabriel was Y'Shua or Yah'shua. Literally translated this means, "YAH saves", and Yah is a contraction of Yahveh."

He stopped pacing and looked at them very seriously. "I encourage you to use the correct names for the God of the universe and His Son. There is power in the proper names. God has permitted the Greek perversion of the true names to continue because He wants each person to be hungry enough to find the truth. I'm sorry, but Jesus has been adopted by the Western world and God will honor its use until a person learns the truth. Now you know the truth. As the Lord himself said "He who has ears to hear, let him hear." Gary then grabbed them both by the hands. "Now let's get down to business."

He gave them both a six-page questionnaire to fill out as truthfully as possible. It covered everything from their parents and grand-parents involvement in all forms of societies to their inner-most feelings on a wide range of subjects. He assured them that no one except himself would ever see their information and that included each other. When Laura objected about that he explained that in many cases there were things such as affairs before a couple met that had never been revealed and some people wanted it to stay that way.

After they completed their forms, Gary retired to a corner of the room and studied them. He then asked Jack to go downstairs and have some coffee while he prayed with Laura. Awhile later the situation was reversed and Laura was sent to the restaurant for an hour.

It was almost midnight by the time they had finished. Jack had been surprised by the demons that had residence within the temple of his body, the people he had to forgive, and things he had to confess to, repent for, rebuke, and pray off of his own life. Gary guided him through the spiritual minefield successfully.

After Jack's session they all met back in their room. Both Jack and Laura felt better than they had for years. Laura was all smiles as they sat down. "I never knew I was carrying so much spiritual baggage."

Jack nodded his agreement. "Bob, do all Christians know about this?"

Gary shook his head. "No and many don't want to know. That's just deception by the devil to keep them in his camp. You would be surprised the number of Christians I have to minister to every year that originally didn't believe that demons could affect a believer, especially ministers and pastors."

The three of them then discussed the Carmelos and what had happened earlier that day. Gary had them repeat their feelings and remembrances one at a time and then sat there praying for insight from the Holy Spirit. After a while he looked up and put his hands on the table.

"I will tell you what I have and see if it makes any sense to you. First, the feelings you had are classic demon of lust patterns. The feeling that the person you are smitten with is the perfect sexual partner for ever and nothing is more critical to your life than being with that person and loving them in every conceivable way. Thinking about it now you see the fallacy of those thoughts. No person can give you satisfaction for more than a few hours in the area of sex. Also, perfect life partners have fights and different personal agendas that make the 'idyllic' life far from achievable. So you can quickly see that the feelings and desires aren't really yours. They were 'impressed' on you and because of your natural sexual nature you assumed they were your own desires." Gary smiled at them. "The sexual nature is the most prolific of Satan's inroads as far as man's fall goes."

"I have a concern though." Gary continued, "The seduction or honey trap is usually slowly applied and very carefully to completely ensnare the victim. A little flesh here and a coy look there and a small kiss, and so on. The building of anticipation is a major factor before each bigger inroad. The fact that they tried to overwhelm you at the first meeting indicates there is a very, very urgent desire to contaminate and control you two. Alan Throman didn't disclose to me what it is that Satan wants with you but it is obviously important to them. Can you enlighten me?" He sat there and waited.

Jack's prayer generated an 'encouragement' to tell Gary about the crucifixion nail in his possession.

Gary asked to see it and Jack went to his briefcase and produced the case. He cautioned the deliverance man to not touch the nail as he had seen first-hand what it could do. Jack realized that there was no power in the object itself but it seemed to polarize the character and beliefs of the person that held it. There were mighty spiritual forces just below the surface that people normally don't tune into. The nail was simply a nexus for such forces.

Gary opened the cover to the box and stared at the rusty-looking nail, more of a spike than a nail. As he looked at it tears came unbidden to his eyes and the agony Christ suffered seemed to become more and more real to him.

Jack carefully took the box away and closed it. Gary was inconsolable for a while and then composed himself. He looked at Jack, "Now we know what the devil wants. How do we handle this situation?"

Laura said, "Well, they originally wanted to give us a message they supposedly received from the Lord. Now we know what 'lord' they got their message from. There must be some importance to the message but it is probably a trap."

Gary thought for a second. "Why don't you get them to come up here and we will confront the demons directly and see if we can't find out what is going on?"

Laura shuddered as she thought of Derrick. "Those evil people, here?"

Gary tipped his head to one side. "Laura" he said quietly. "Those people are God-fearing Christians that have fallen under the control of evil forces. They themselves are not evil, they are being used for evil and it would be in their favor if we can 'deliver' them from this control."

Jack agreed, "Then we could find out what they know."

Gary laughed. "They probably don't know anything. They are probably not even aware that they are not still in Greece. But the demons controlling them could be a mine of information."

Laura looked at Gary strangely, "I thought that you weren't supposed to involve yourself with demons. It just gives them more power doesn't it?"

Gary shook his head slowly. "Not in my case. I told you that the Holy Spirit anointed me to do battle. The down side of that privilege is that I must do battle, not avoid it. I will be able to find out what you need to know and probably eliminate the demons cursing the Carmelos. Just beware that the demons will not like it when they see me. But, I will get the truth, trust me."

CHAPTER THIRTY-ONE

Jack's call was answered by Katherine. Her voice was still warm and silky-smooth but it had lost its total attraction that it once had. Jack acted like he was still silly as a goose about her and purposely neglected to ask to talk to Derrick. After a minute of inane conversation she asked him what it was he wanted. He implied she knew what he wanted, which resulted in warm laughter. Then he asked if they could come over to the hotel where Jack was staying in an hour. He asked her if she would like to come over a while earlier by herself. Again the laughter, but she was adamant that both she and Derrick needed to come over together. She implied that Derrick would keep Laura far too busy to worry about her and Jack. She whispered a sultry "I'll be with you soon." and hung up.

Jack looked over at Gary and Laura who had been listening on an extension. Laura looked grim and Gary looked very serious. He came over and told them both, "We need some *serious* prayer before they get here. She almost got to me! And she wasn't even aware I was on the line."

Gary led the prayers for the next forty-five minutes and by the time there was a knock on the door they were prepared. Jack went to the door and opened it. Katherine came in first and hugged Jack. She adroitly made sure every curve she had made contact with his body. He hugged her back and stood aside for Derrick who made a bee-line for Laura. Jack closed the door and locked it. Then Gary came out of the bedroom into the sitting room. Things changed dramatically.

Derrick looked furious, "How can you let that man near you? He's a vile, etc. etc. Derrick soon ran out of words when he saw that the whole thing was a set up. Gary walked up to Derrick and said, "Sit down!" Derrick immediately sat down on the chair next to him. Gary sat down across from him. Gary looked him directly in the eyes and said, "What is your name?"

It was obvious to everyone that the real game was known and sham wasn't going to cut it anymore. In a voice that definitely didn't belong to such a beautiful man the demon controlling Derrick said, "Lust and I have a right to this man. You can't do anything about it either!"

Gary sat unperturbed. "Why do you have a right to him?"

The demon didn't say a word.

Gary prayed, "Yahshua I ask you to assign two of your mighty angels to torment this demon of lust until he answers truthfully the questions I ask him in your name."

Derrick started to squirm and writhe. "No, NO, NO, Stop! All right! I'll answer your questions."

Gary asked him what his assignment was beyond seducing the Malones.

Lust answered, "Nothing, we were just to get them to sin with these bodies and then, others, would attend to them."

Gary waited for the Holy Spirit to confirm that answer. He didn't get a confirmation. "Yahshua, help me get the truth from this spirit!"

Derrick went through a series of jerks and facial expressions. "All right, we were supposed to lead them to the hidden headquarters of the real leaders of the ASF in Syria.

Gary asked, "For what purpose?"

Derrick hung his head, "To force them to give up the treasure."

"Is that all?"

Derrick nodded his head. The pride of the demon came forth. "It was a really simple assignment."

Gary told Lust in the name of Yahshua to go down and let him talk to the real Derrick. After a struggle he did as he was told and the real Derrick looked at Gary in confusion. "What's going on?" He looked around, "Where am I?"

Gary quickly told him what the situation was and asked him if he wanted to be free of the demonic powers which were riding him. He eagerly agreed and Gary went to work. It wasn't easy but in the end four different demons were consigned to the abyss until Yahshua returned at the end of the world to judge the living and the dead.

Katherine seemed to shrink into herself and huddled near the wall on the floor. Jack's instructions were to make sure she didn't interfere or escape. She didn't.

Gary sat Derrick down and had Jack sit across from him and pray for the infilling of the Holy Spirit. Gary and Laura confronted Katherine. Having seen how things went with Derrick it was much easier with her. The six demons controlling her life left without much of a fight. But the leader, which was again a demon of lust, gave them some interesting information.

After considerable prayer and a few phone calls to Greece, the Carmelos shook hands all around and left for the airport. They weren't even going to go near the hotel where the demons had them staying.

After they left, Laura caught Jack shaking his head. When she asked him what that was about he replied, "They are actually a couple of really nice people. I noticed that without the demon of lust there was no interest for any of us."

Gary nodded his head and rubbed the back of his neck. It was almost noon on Saturday and the prayer session was set for six p.m. He was fasting and hadn't slept for two days and had been hard at it for the last six hours. Laura suggested he get a few hours of sleep in the extra bed in the room and they would wake him in time for the prayer session.

Before lying down though he made a summary for both Jack and Laura. It was pretty much as he had expected. Both Derrick and Katherine were into affairs outside of their marriage and had opened the doors wide for the demons. The demons made them think that they were doing normal things while they were actually being used for the demon's purposes.

"When you walk away from God to fulfill an appetite, you open yourself up to a roomful of trouble. Remember that. Also, the demon controlling Katherine mentioned a superior demon named Uthoth. Think of this demon like an Archangel on the other side. Satan patterns his demons like God does the angels. This Uthoth is the guiding force behind the attack on you. His orders are to produce results quickly because there is something important coming up that makes his boss want that crucifixion nail really bad." Gary continued, "Also, I'm only guessing here, but I think the entire poisoning of the world was done to maneuver you and the nail into his hands."

Jack sat there for several minutes trying to understand the implications of Gary's last statement. "You mean this demon, Uthoth, would deliberately kill tens of millions of people just to get control of the nail?"

Gary nodded, "Oh sure. Remember, their charter is to kill, steal, and destroy. This would be a double coup for him to do both."

Jack sat there with his head down. "That means I am responsible for all the people who might die from this horrible Mad Cow disease, right?"

Gary put his hand on Jack's shoulder. "God doesn't allow the dark forces to use his children that way. Go to God with your concern. I personally don't think it mattered what they did to get that nail. They will continue to try to destroy mankind one at a time or by the millions until the end."

Laura gave Gary a blanket and pillow and he stretched out for some sleep.

Jack went into the bedroom and got on his knees. The peace of Christ soon filled him and he understood much more clearly the responsibility of protecting God's treasures. He also found that he wasn't responsible for the poisoning. Katherine's demon had lied to misdirect Gary in hopes it would spread dissension in their ranks. Now he didn't feel guilty, only mad. That also made him wonder how much of what they had learned was true.

CHAPTER THIRTY-TWO

David walked up the Messianic Synagogue's stairs to the dressing room and found Sarah talking to the Rabbi. Seeing David, she got up and came over to him. She asked, "What is the latest on the television coverage?"

David smiled and told her to sit down. He motioned the Rabbi to join them. "It seems that God is in this as you expected. Not only are all the broadcast and cable stations in Israel going to cover the prayer session, it seems that they have been monitoring and reporting on the prayer fast, too. But, that is not all. I heard from President Bollen's staff a few minutes ago that the concept of the fast and prayer to heal the unsaved, but contaminated, caught on big in the U.S. In fact, according to my information, CNN and every other world media have been championing the fast and prayer as the only hope for tens of millions of Americans as well as our people. They are set as direct links from the Israeli media on a real-time, synchronized coverage for the prayer session this evening." He watched the awe on Sarah's face with happiness.

Sarah thought for a few seconds, "It will be between eight a.m. and eleven a.m. across America. That will allow millions of believers to pray together. Wonderful!"

David reached out and took her hand. "Are you worried about leading the whole world in prayer?"

Sarah was alright, "No, not at all. I really doubt that I'll be the one speaking with my mouth anyway. But, just in case I've got my notes ready. Oh, David this is wonderful."

David agreed and checked his watch. Just five hours until the broadcast. "Did you see that Christi Steel has changed her concert to a 'pre-prayer' program that will lead up to your session? She's got two giant TV screens so that everyone in the arena can watch and pray with you."

Sarah shook her head, "No, I didn't think that was what her 'entertainment' or her fans were about."

David nodded, "Don't forget, her niche is 'Christian Rock' and what could be more Christian than supporting a prayer session to save the lost?"

"What are Jack and Laura doing right now?" Sarah looked over at Mark who was reading a Bible in a comfortable seat in the corner.

Mark looked up from his reading, "I don't know exactly, but I do know that they have been fasting and will be at the studio to support you for the session."

At the same time Sarah was asking Mark where the Malones were, Jack was working with Gary Eisenthal on the Internet looking for information on 'Uthoth' or Syrian news that could indicate where this particular brand of evil was located.

Gary explained "When a demon like Uthoth is in a certain area, the incidences of violence, depravity, and immorality accelerate and are usually reported as a local phenomenon by the local press."

After twenty minutes it was obvious where this particular brand of sickness was staying. Gary pointed out the increase in homicides, suicides, and domestic violence in the last four months in the tiny, almost obscure town of Bosra ash Sham near the Jordanian border.

Laura was sitting in a chair near the windows. "What are we going to do if we can get to Bosra?"

Gary frowned. "Well, there are one or two things we can try. First is find a person who is obviously demonized and simply let Uthoth know that we are there to see him. Second, and better, is to pray for God's covering and go locate him without his knowing we are there. Then we can confront him directly without his having time to prepare."

Jack had been watching Gary throughout the time he had been with them. He was able to discern patterns to the way things needed to be done in the realm of spiritual warfare. "Then we ask the Holy Spirit to show us where to go and how to find this creature, right?"

Gary held up his hand. "First, we pray to see if this is what the Lord wants us to do. I have never confronted a demon of Archangel Potential. If God isn't behind us one-hundred percent we had better not challenge him."

Jack agreed and suggested that they also pray for the prayer session about to start. Sarah is going to need a solid covering if she is going to lead this worldwide prayer without interference from the enemy."

"We can be intercessors for her and you're right, she is going to need the best defense we can ask the Lord for to keep the enemy away." Gary concurred. "I'm also sure that the church here in Israel has many Intercessors praying for her and the coverage and the studio and everything they can think of at this time."

CHAPTER THIRTY-THREE

Christi finished the last number to a tremendous ovation. She made sure the band took a bow and shared in the fan's adoration. Carefully checking the time she saw that they had time for one more song before the beginning of the prayer session.

She had rewritten her original hit of "ArchAngel Fire" to take in the poisoning situation in Israel and the U.S. and made it almost military in its rising beat and wording. She had carefully prepared the music to reach this point at this time and as the band jammed out the first bars of the song, the crowd went wild. It was a good, loud, back beat that kept the whole thing together but it had been God who put the words in her heart and mind. As the rendition spelled out the horror and pain of the disease the crowd settled down and became quiet so as to hear the lyrics.

As she finished the song there was total silence in the arena and she spoke from her heart to the overflow crowd. "I wrote this for everyone who has the disease and who is about to be cured of it by Yahshua! Now I am going to turn the monitors over to the prayer session beginning here in Israel and I want each and every one of you to join in the prayer with me."

She motioned and the monitors winked and the inside of the studio set came into view. It was a good rendition of a church altar and had a large cross hanging just behind the altar.

Exactly at 6:00 p.m. Tel Aviv time, Music began to play and it was an uplifting theme that stirred the hearts of all that heard it. The music swelled and one could feel great and wonderful things were just around the corner. It affected people all over the world.

In homes throughout Israel and the United States people got down on their knees and realized that if God was there and willing to hear their pleas it was time to ask for Holy help with the illness that was killing them.

The music fell to a light background as Sarah approached the dais and turned to the cameras and the people in the room. She was dressed in a simple white smock with a small red cross below her throat. Her hair was covered with a white cloth that hung down to her arms. She knelt down at the altar and said a silent prayer for guidance and strength. She looked up at the TV camera and spoke.

"To the people of Israel, United States of America, and the rest of the world. The cruel and vicious act by a small group of fanatical people has endangered millions of God's children. Yes, regardless of your religious beliefs or leanings, you are all God's children and he loves you."

"Tonight, we who are His servants will pray that he heals all people of this horrible disease to His glory and honor. I will use a prayer from the King James Bible that is based on the book of Daniel, ninth chapter, sixteenth verse. The words will be displayed in your language at the bottom of the screen. First, we will ask the Lord to cleanse us. Then I will ask you to pray the way I was told to just before the Lord performed a miracle before my eyes. I will repeat the instructions I was given then. "Do not doubt! Do not let religious differences hinder you. Pray with your heart, not your head." Christian believers do not have the disease and that is because we each asked Him to heal us. Tonight, millions of believers will ask God to heal those that haven't, for whatever reason, turned to Him. This is Intercessory prayer for the stricken people. We must forgive the afflicted because God has forgiven us of all our sins."

Sarah stood to her feet and raised her hands. "Dear Lord Yahshua, cleanse me with the atoning blood you shed in seven places before and at Calvary for the remission of our sins. I am a sinner Lord, and I ask you to forgive me so that I can raise holy hands to you." She stood there for a few seconds and then began to pray."

"O Lord, according to all thy righteousness, I beseech thee, let thy anger and thy fury be turned away from the people of the Earth: because for our sins, and for the iniquities of our fathers, many of thy people have become poisoned and will surely die. Now therefore, O Father God we thy servants beseech thee to hear our prayers, our supplications, and cause thy face to shine upon thy people which are desolate, for the Lord's sake. O my God, incline thy ear, and hear, open thy eyes, and behold our desolations: for we do not present our supplications before thee for our righteousness, but for thy great mercies for everyone stricken with this disease from the enemy. O Lord, hear; O Lord, forgive; O Lord, hearken and do; defer not, for thy own sake, O my God: heal thy people to the glory and honor of thy name."

Sarah paused for a short time and then made one last statement. "Dear, sweet, precious Yahshua, who sits at the right hand of the Father, interceding for us, we pray all this in your glorious name and we thank you for your mercy."

She then turned and walked away from the altar.

The whole world held its breath to see if God would turn His anger and fury away and heal His people. Many people felt the conviction of God and knew in their hearts that He would save them. The vast majority weren't sure. They hoped and waited. Many felt that God couldn't, or wouldn't do anything about their distress.

Across America people wondered and debated the purposes and mercy of the God of the Universe in their own terms, while they waited to find out their fate.

People begin to filter into the testing stations as soon as they opened, early as 6:00 pm on Saturday, in response to the demand after the prayer. Within thirty minutes, reports began to reach the media that every infected person tested showed no sign of the disease.

In a side note, researchers could not find any sign of the poison they had been working on in their laboratories. It simply had ceased to exist anywhere in the world. Later attempts to recreate it were useless. It was like it had never existed.

CHAPTER THIRTY-FOUR

The jubilation and celebrations continued throughout the world and especially in America where eighteen million people had been given a reprieve by God. But it was a definite warning that few would forget.

The celebration in Israel was muted due to the source of the salvation. Many prayers of thanks were given to God and the debate over the reality of Yahshua being "the Messiah" was forever changed. This would alter the religious landscape of Israel, but it would take time. The major reason was the entrenched thinking that a Messiah was yet to come for Israel. The younger generations had no problem connecting the solution to the person of Yahshua. This in itself was to cause much debate in families and Synagogues throughout the land.

Against this jubilant background, Jack placed a serious call to David Zahavy at Mossad headquarters. When the connection was completed, Jack explained, "We have to investigate a possible tie-in to the poisoning and the terrorists and we need your help."

Since it was almost 11 a.m. in Tel Aviv, David suggested that they get together for lunch at the Malone's hotel.

After David and Sarah were seated they had ordered drinks in the up-scale eatery, it wasn't hard to understand why they didn't ask for the water.

Then, Jack introduced Gary Eisenthal to them and explained the events of the last two days involving the Carmelos. Sarah cocked her head as Jack described his "imposed" feeling about Katherine Carmelos. She smiled at Laura and slightly rolled her eyes. Laura just shook her head. When Jack got to the message they were programmed to give him and Laura, David asked him to go over it again.

"I got this from Katherine the first night, but wasn't thinking too straight and remembered even less. The same message was pried out of the demon of lust that was controlling her. It goes like this. The three real masterminds of the ASF escaped capture because no one knows who they are. They are hiding out in a house in Bosra, Syria. The Carmelos, guided by their demons were to direct us to the right place, but that is no longer an option."

David looked at Gary but asked Jack, "Why not just contact the President and have U.S. troops find these 'leaders'?"

Jack shook his head. "I don't know who they are, what they look like, or even where in Bosra they are. Also, there is a tie-in with us. There is an Archangel-level demon named 'Uthoth' that was behind the poisoning and behind the scheme to get us there."

Gary added, "There seems to be some great urgency involved with this move of Satan. I have been praying about this and I get the impression that a small group of us need to go to Bosra and confront this Uthoth. It is highly probable that he is being hosted by one of the ASF leaders."

That got David's interest. "How are you going to locate this spirit?"

Gary took the question. "We will get to the town and rely on the leading of the Holy Spirit. I am certain He will lead us to the demon."

Sarah was ruefully smiling and glanced at David. She raised her eyebrows and tipped her head toward the team.

David nodded his head. "All right, let us assume you are right and it is a small band that needs to go. There are some significant hurtles to surmount before you get there." He sat back and ticked them off his fingers. "First, you are talking about Syria. Syria has no love for Israel. You cannot even enter Syria if your passport has been stamped by Israel. Second, there are severe, and I do mean severe, penalties for illegally entering the country, carrying a firearm without a Syrian license, or drinking alcohol. Once you get there you will face a potentially hostile population and equally possibly, a portion of the Syrian army. Lastly, Americans and Christians are only slightly less hated than the Jewish people."

Mark looked at David, "Your point?"

David laughed. "Yes, Mark, I know that everything I said is almost normal operating procedure for you." He sat there thinking for a while. Then he sat up and said, "If you want to risk all these dangers, I can get you into Syria and even to Bosra without being detected. I can also supply you with Soviet weapons so they can't be traced to us or the United States. But there are two conditions on this assistance." He looked around at the team.

"First, you have to be in and out in less than ten hours. Everything could easily break down after that point and we would have the entire Syrian army on top of us. Second, you allow me to accompany you."

Laura shrugged her shoulders, "No problem, why break up a good team anyway?"

The planning only took an hour with a great deal of work to be done by David and Sarah after they returned to the office. They scheduled the time to cross the border as 4 a.m. since that was the quietest hour when sentries were at their least attentiveness.

CHAPTER THIRTY-FIVE

Having sought the Lord on His will concerning this venture, the team assembled at a remote military airbase near the Israeli-Jordanian, border close to the Dead Sea, at one o'clock in the morning.

Gary Eisenthal explained what he thought they would encounter. "When we get to Bosra we will seek the Holy Spirit and the will of God to locate the host body of this Uthoth demon. We will find him I assure you. The Lord is behind this venture and He will place us where we need to be. Once we find him we will have to rely on the Holy Spirit to lead us as to what to do."

Gary took a second and made sure he had their undivided attention, especially David and Sarah. "We haven't had time to go over your 'spiritual balance' and I don't know if you have vulnerabilities that this demon could use. Since the two of you will be with the group that confronts this spirit, you need to be as 'bullet-proof' as possible. In the next few hours I will work with you both as new Christians to ensure your spiritual safety."

He paced back and forth a couple times while he composed his words. "What we are going up against is only a demon. Yahshua defeated the demons when he defeated Satan at the cross. He also gave us, as His disciples, the power over all demons."

Sarah raised her hand and halted his discourse. "What exactly are demons and what do they want?"

Gary replied, "Most Christian thought says that demons are fallen angels who joined Satan in his rebellion against God and were cast down to Earth with Satan when he was thrown out of heaven. That they are now evil spirits under Satan's control. There are theories that demons are the spiritual component of the people who lived on the Earth before the flood that Noah survived."

Sarah cocked her head to one side, "Why them?"

Gary sat down and spread his hands. "I don't know exactly because God has not revealed it to me, but as I understand it, God became angry with the people on Earth after Adam caused the fall of mankind and literally gave the control of the Earth to Satan. Satan was able to release many of the fallen angels from the 'pit' at that time, in an attempt to thwart God's plan for man. It is probable that the increase of human sin helped release them then, just as it is doing today in the world. Satan had the fallen angels mate with human women to produce 'corrupt' seed. God was very disappointed and had decided to wipe the Earth clean of the 'immoral' people. The only 'clean' seed he found on Earth was Noah and his family. That is why God instructed him to build the Ark and save his family, the birds, and land animals to start the human race over again."

"But the children of the fallen angels had an evil spiritual component, which survived in the spirit world, that heaven and hell are a part of, after their death. Some people think that these are the source of demons. All spirits are eternal, both the good and the evil."

Gary shrugged his shoulders. "It doesn't really matter to me. I just know that they help Satan tempt people to sin and have great destructive powers. But whenever they are confronted by Yahshua, they lose their power."

Gary continued, "In Luke 9:1 Yahshua gave his disciples authority over demons. I quote *"When Yahshua had called the Twelve together, he gave them power and authority to drive out all demons."* Also, in Luke 10:17-19, He gave even more people this authority. Again I'm quoting, *"The seventy-two returned with joy and said, "Lord, even the demons submit to us in your name." He replied, "I have given you authority to trample on snakes and scorpions and to overcome all the power of the enemy; nothing will harm you."* So Yahshua Himself tells you that as his follower, or disciple, you have the power over the enemy in His name. The operative words are 'His name'. We must be acting in accordance to His will and realize we have absolutely no power of our own concerning this spiritual domain. So you see, while you are powerless in yourself, as a representative of Yahshua you have power over the demons, as the Lord cautions though. *."..Do not rejoice that the spirits submit to you, but rejoice that your names are written in heaven."* "You see, Yahshua knew how easily Satan can fool men into sinning, especially by pride. His caution was against taking pride in power over demons. He told the seventy-two that had returned claiming victory over the enemy, *"I saw Satan fall like lightning from heaven. Yours is the kind of pride that led to Satan's downfall, be careful"*

He sat down and looked at the assembled team. "Do be careful to guard your hearts from pride. This Uthoth is a craftier, smarter, and more dangerous demon than the normal ones. I have never faced this level of enemy, other than corporately, with others more skilled than myself. We must all be careful." He got up and motioned Mark, David, and Sarah to follow him. Jack saw forms like the ones he and Laura had filled out in Gary's hands and heard Mark ask as they left, "Gary, why do you use Yahshua rather than Jesus?"

Later, Mark walked up to the two Force Recon Marines and discussed the more earthly, military plan. "Craig, you, Kevin, and myself will provide the physical security for these guys as they meet with this demon. We will all assume a perimeter defense and I will act as high guard with the scoped rifle since I used to do this type of thing back in the SEALs. Craig you will control the left flank and also watch our rear. Kevin, you will handle the right flank and watch for aircraft or land vehicles that could interfere."

Mark walked over to a table loaded with equipment. "Like normal we are going in overloaded but with sufficient firepower to stop three squads if we have to." He hoisted a rifle so that they could see it. "I'm sure you're familiar with the Soviet version of the AK54." They both nodded their heads. "Okay" Mark said as he put the rifle down. "We are going to have two hundred rounds each for the rifles. This is an RPG, again something I think you have trained with, as well as five rounds for each of two launchers."

He went on and detailed the Soviet night vision gear, grenades, anti-personnel mines similar to the Claymore, radio gear, and Soviet concentrated ration packs. "These I doubt that you've tried and I can tell you now, that they are not up to the standards of MREs (meals ready to eat) that the U.S. supplies its troops."

Kevin made a face. "How about we have a twelve-hour fast?"

Mark laughed softly, "Sure. I don't plan to eat one unless we end up being there longer than we're supposed to be."

At that point the three men started to field-strip the rifles and clean them.

Jack and Laura went off by themselves a short distance away from the camp and talked. Jack hugged his young wife, "Honey, I realize this is a little more complicated than arranging for a dinner party, and possibly a little more dangerous. But, I'm proud that you are going and want you to know that I couldn't do it without you."

Laura hugged him back. "This doesn't seem so bad. Let's see, we are going to illegally enter an Arab country at the ungodly hour of four a.m., for which the penalty is life imprisonment. Confront an upper level demon, for which the penalty could be eternal damnation. Bring Russian military weapons into said Arab country, for which the penalty is death by firing squad. Go into a Muslim enclave as Christians and in the company of Israelis, for which the penalty is possibly being stoned to death."

She stepped away from him and turned to look at his face in the dim moonlight on the desert. "Does that about cover it? I would say our dance cards are full, wouldn't you?"

Jack thought about that for a minute. "You know, I really never looked at this that way. Do you want to return to Tel Aviv?"

She shook her head. "I want us both to go home and live a normal life. But, I have made a deal with the Lord. He tells me what to do and I'll do it." She stepped into his arms and finished her statement with her face buried against his chest. "He wants me to go with you. He also wants us to face this 'Uthoth' in Bosra. So that is what I will do. I also am happy to be with you regardless what we are doing." She leaned back and studied his face. "I would never have guessed I would be living the life of a female Rambo in foreign countries and dealing with jet fighters, atomic bombs, mass poisonings, terrorists, or demons. But it's going to look great on my resume!"

Jack laughed and took her hand to walk back to the camp. "Come on, Rambette; let's get a few minutes rest before we have to get down to business."

CHAPTER THIRTY-SIX

Everyone geared up, which included packs and loads for the ladies to help distribute the gear on the way to Basra. In the pre-dawn dark they were led out to a hanger in which stood one of the strangest jets Jack had ever seen. He nudged Mark, "What type of aircraft is this?"

Mark shook his head. "I don't know. I thought I was up on all the varieties of combat aircraft in the world but I've never seen anything quite like this."

The craft was painted in sandy camouflage and had stubby wings with large humps in the center of the wings. It was about fifty feet long and only about ten high. It wasn't sitting on wheels but on feet and had another large, sandy-colored hump toward the rear of the chassis. The back of the craft sported two stubby wings with short tails on them. The whole thing was obviously designed as stealthy with only front windows raked back at an extreme angle and angles around the upper surfaces to misdirect radar.

David waved everyone up the single step into the fuselage. There were fifteen jump seats on each side of the fuselage and a storage area for gear in the rear. After everyone racked their gear and strapped into the seats the crew of two locked the door and went up front. There was a very muted whine from accelerating turbofan jet engines and then the craft lifted off of its feet and hovered in the hanger.

Mark raised his eyebrows at David. David smiled. "I didn't think you would know about this aircraft. Very, very few people do. This is what we call a Sand Snake. The operating altitude for the Sand Snake is eight feet. It is primarily an air-cushion vehicle pushed by jet engines and travels very quickly and very quietly across the desert. We are going to cross into Jordan and go south of Amman. We will go into Syria about 100 miles and turn north by northwest. We will then go about fifty miles to the outskirts of Bosra."

Mark scowled, "How can you zip across the desert without being detected by high or low tech observers?"

"Because we don't go near any observers," was his reply.

At the questioning look he got in reply to that, David continued to describe their means of transportation. "This vehicle is computer controlled and guided by a combination of satellite and AWACS inputs. It is very quiet, doesn't raise a great deal of a sand track and is highly maneuverable. The satellite data shows any possible contacts and then they determine the best path to avoid those contacts. The camouflage paint and the low altitude prevent anyone that is within a mile of the path from seeing anything. There are times when we have to lie doggo on the sand for a time to clear complicated contacts, but that is rare because the desert is a large place and is primarily uninhabited."

Jack asked David, "What are they waiting on?"

David sat back in his seat, "For a good satellite position that will cover our entire trip without lapses."

No more than had he said the words and the Sand Snake began to glide out of the hanger in the dark. As the craft left the vicinity of the airbase it began to pick up a frightening forward velocity. Laura hung on to her seat and told everyone, "I'm glad I can't see out. I think it would scare me to death!" There was no laughter at that point.

Mark quipped to David, "You don't think they'd make a mistake and go to Basra in Iraq do you?"

David stared at Mark for a few seconds and then realized he was being ribbed. He chuckled and reached up to flip a switch that activated two monitors on the front bulkhead. One was a computer enhancement of the satellite view of their mission. The desired path was a thin green line that primarily went straight but had some curves and jogs in it. The actual travel was a fatter white line making its way along the green one. Red points and circles showed the contacts to avoid and a color variation showed the surface elevation. The second was an enhanced video of their forward travel.

It was an exciting ride and only took forty minutes from the time they left the hanger to violate two foreign nation's borders and approach Basra, Syria.

The Sand Snake slowed to a halt about a mile from the town and for several seconds blasted its lift repulse fans very hard, but still almost silently. Sand flew in all directions. The engines died out and the craft settled into the small depression at the base of a sand dune it had just created.

Everybody geared up and checked each other's loads. David nodded to the crewman by the door and it was opened. The cool dry desert air surged into the body of the vehicle and evaporated the sweat off of more than one brow.

Jumping from the doorway one by one the team left the side of the craft and the door was closed. They walked about fifty feet away in the shifting sand and stopped.

The vast expanse of the desert was felt in the silence and quiet beauty of the landscape. A quarter-moon was dropping toward the horizon and it lent a surreal atmosphere to the little gathering on the sand. It seemed like all eternity stretched out in all directions. Laura thought about the forty days that Yahshua spent in the desert after he was baptized. This scene impressed upon her that the lonely desert would definitely be a place to meet God and learn about Him. There was little to distract you. There was only a slight breeze in the cool air that moved her hair in miniature gusts.

Looking back at the Sand Snake she was impressed. Unless you knew exactly where the craft was, you couldn't find it. In the pale moonlight, it blended into the shadows of the sand and being half buried in the side of the dune it didn't present a shape to locate. The team turned and hurried on through the quiet desert so as to be in the town by the time the sun came up.

CHAPTER THIRTY-SEVEN

As they approached the city from the southwest, David put up his right fist. Everybody melted into the sand and trained their weapons forward. David spoke a word in Arabic. The response was also a single word. David rose and walked forward to meet a man who appeared out of the gloom. Sarah nudged Jack, "That's one of our in-place agents."

The agent led them single file to a building on the outskirts of the small town. Basra appeared to live up to its reputation. It was an obscure little tourist town with one good hotel and one big attraction about ninety miles in the desert south of Damascus. The whole town is built on, or around, old Roman buildings. The entire city seemed to be made of black basalt that had been torn off of older buildings. There was a large Roman Theatre/Citadel that dominated the town (the attraction). The building they entered was not much more than an elaborate shed but it kept the elements out.

Gary and David were in heavy discussions with the agent while the rest of the team kept a low profile and watched the area around the building from the few windows and the doorway. David rejoined the group and Gary came in right behind him. David showed them a map of the city. "As is to be expected, this demon is probably located in the nicest place that's hard to get to around here." He indicated a building on the map. He looked at his watch. "We have about twenty minutes to get there before everybody starts moving around, but the problem is that it seems nobody is there right now. What do we do?"

Gary and Laura said almost in unison, "Pray."

As a group they knelt and prayed for guidance. Jack finally looked up and spoke for the group. "David, can we remain here until this evening? I definitely feel we are in the right place but the time isn't quite right yet. Does that violate the ten hour maximum?"

David thought for a minute and went back and conferred with the agent. After some discussion they were led to an area in the back of the building and a hidden trapdoor was opened. They filed into a small underground tunnel that led to a large, poorly lit and inadequately ventilated room with a low ceiling. They dropped their gear and settled down to wait. David brought out a communicator and was able to reach the Sand Snake and request the delay which was approved.

After the pre-combat jitters it was hard to unwind. Everybody tried to rest or sleep but it wasn't working. Mark was concerned about being trapped like rats in the cellar and wished they were where they could see what was going on around them. David urged him to rest. The wait had dragged on for what seemed like a small eternity when they heard someone coming down the ladder and into the tunnel. It was the in-place agent. He motioned for them to come back up. They picked up their gear and as quietly as possible climbed back into the house above them.

Against Mark's expectations there were no people with guns waiting for them. It was about seven p.m. local time and there was little or no night life in the town. David identified the smells of mezzah or pre-meal snacks, Arabic unleavened bread, or khobz that filled the air. Other smells indicated some people were eating felafel, deep-fried chickpea balls; shwarma, spit-cooked sliced lamb; and fuul, a paste of fava beans, garlic and lemon.

This reminded everyone that they hadn't eaten in a while, but were getting wound up for possible combat again, let them ignore the hunger pangs, that and the thought of the Russian rations. The agent led them through back alleys and quiet streets to the building they had targeted. There were lights on in the building and guards out front.

Seeing the guards, Mark reconsidered his planning. He turned to Craig, "You've done some sniper work?"

Craig nodded.

Mark handed him the sniper rifle. "You take the high spot. I think I'm going to be needed inside. The inclusion of the military guards bothers me."

Craig agreed and they rearranged their coverage.

David sent the agent away so he would not compromise his cover. Then Sarah and Kevin disappeared into the gloom. A minute later the two guards also disappeared and Kevin flashed a penlight to get them to join him. At this point Craig and Kevin dispersed to provide coverage while the other six hid their packs and walked into the courtyard and to the front door of the house.

Since sneaking around would probably be a waste of time anyway, Jack tried the doorknob and the door opened without resistance. One would expect that of a door guarded by sentries. All six people walked into a large entry hall with a high ceiling. Through the door to the left they heard conversation so they went that way.

Opening the door to a large room without furniture, the team entered and walked into the room. They couldn't hear the people talking anymore and the room seemed deserted. The door slammed shut with a bang behind them and they heard a very low and evil chuckle. Gary held up both his hands and said, "Everyone pray that the Lord protect you and give you wisdom as to what is going on."

The lighting in the room dimmed considerably and the members of the team moved closer together and watched in all directions at once. For several minutes nothing else happened.

Laura prayed silently for wisdom and protection. She reviewed her "armor" from the helmet of salvation to the sword of the Word and found herself as prepared as possible. She suddenly saw a mental image of a bottomless pit and a trapdoor. "Gary! I saw a picture of a trapdoor with a pit below it. This room could be that trap!"

Gary nodded his head. Taking out the combat knife he had been issued he said, "Quickly, find a wall and give yourself a hook to hang on!"

Each of the team followed suit and ran to the wall behind them and slammed their knives into the paneling with both hands. Jack felt a little foolish when the floor didn't drop out from below him.

Less than a second after that, the floor did exactly that. The entire floor of the room hinged at the ends and fell open. Jack, Mark, and David fell about two feet with their knives slicing through the paneling due to their weight. Jack felt a sinking feeling in his gut as he started to fall. Then he realized it didn't bother him that much because live or die he knew God was in control of his life and future. But, all three of them came up against a cross stud and their knife blades dug into it and held at that point. Due to their lighter weight the other three members knives held in the original position where they had been stabbed into the wall.

The situation wasn't greatly improved because their arm muscles were tiring from hanging all their weight on their hands. Mark looked around for a solution but everything was too far away from his position to reach. He looked over at Sarah to find her smiling back at him. That made him feel better and he realized that he could find a solution. Keeping his knife securely imbedded in the wood of the cross brace he carefully pulled his right foot back and shot it forward into the paneling above where the floor would have been normally. His combat boot smashed a hole in the paneling and two more kicks made a large enough hole he could put his foot on the wooden stud revealed by the hole. He then put his foot on the stud and let go his right hand from the handle of the knife.

Smashing another hole above the cross stud he was able to secure a hand hold on the cross stud. Securely planted now, he smashed two more holes with his other foot and hand and then pulled his knife out of the wall and plunged it through the outer wall beyond his right hand. Twisting the blade created a larger hole. Some more knife work opened a large hole into the hallway they had been in before entering the room. Sheathing his knife he reached through the outer hole and started disassembling the wall panel out there.

Mark was in excellent physical shape and his upper body strength was exceptional. He soon had a hole big enough to get through. He carefully determined where everybody else was hanging and said, "Hang on. I'll be there in a minute." With that he pulled himself up and out through the hole and disappeared from the bottomless room.

Several seconds later a knife blade appeared above Sarah's knife blade and described a large but sloppy hole. A crunch shook the paneling as the hole was knocked out past Sarah and Mark leaned out through the hole. Grabbing both of Sarah's wrists he pulled her up and into the hole. Her belt got hung up on her knife handle and it took a few seconds to free her and retrieve the knife. Then her feet disappeared from the view of the other four people. Mark's head reappeared and he estimated distances.

The ragged-hole routine was repeated over Laura's position and Gary's at the same time. Sarah reached out and pulled Laura into the hole above her knife while Mark repeated the operation for Gary. Less than two minutes later David and Jack were rescued in the same fashion.

As the team sat on the floor of the hall and massaged their aching arm muscles Gary prayed their thankfulness to a God that didn't abandon them in their time of need. He then got up and shook Mark's hand.

Sarah was looking around the hall. "What now?"

Indicating the only other door in the hall Jack said, "Why don't we try that one?"

Laura suggested that only one at a time try that door. Mark seconded that with "I like the way the lady thinks."

Reassembling into a group Jack opened the second door. This was a more conventional room with furniture in it. Still, they proceeded carefully across the room to one of the two doors set in the back wall of the room.

Mark opened the left door and it was simply a closet. He closed the door and tried the right one. Slamming the door shut he turned his back to it and closed his eyes. Sarah reached out and touched his hand, "What is it?"

Mark shook his head and looked ill. "It is . . . horrible!" Don't go in there. Better yet, don't open that door!" He was very emphatic about it.

Gary moved up next to Mark. "Mark, this is a house of deception and evil. You can't be sure of anything. What did you see that filled you with such horror?"

Mark shook his head, "The room is an abattoir. It is filled with the bodies of children all ripped apart in the cruelest fashion. The fear and terror is still on their faces. I've never seen anything so disgustingly horrid!"

Gary slowly nodded his head. "I'm sure you haven't. But then that is exactly why you saw what you did. If I, or any of the others here, looked into the room we would probably see the thing that is the most horrible to us. Your love for children and their protection is what probably keyed that vision."

With that, Gary confidently strode to the door and opened it. He saw other things equally gruesome but since he knew they were imaginary, he dismissed it as reality, and boldly stated, "I rebuke this room in the mighty name of Yahshua. I call upon the Angels of God to bind up every demon in this room and to cast them into the abyss to the end of time, never to return, in the name of Yahshua!" He then walked into the room. Mark narrowed his eyes and followed the slighter man. One by one the other four entered the room and found themselves in another entranceway and hall.

Laura shook her head. "This place is a maze like the wormholes they give you in software games."

Gary nodded his head, "Holy Spirit, guide us from this maze and to the confrontation that our Heavenly Father wants us to complete."

A few seconds later the conversation could be heard again behind another doorway off the hall. Carefully opening the door, Mark looked into the room and signaled the others to follow him.

The team quietly slid into a large room filled with Rattan furniture and the solid Arabic decor of a movie set.

Three men were seated around a low table talking when the central figure noticed the uninvited guests. The two men to the sides were surprised and obviously upset. They were nondescript personages, small men without any really outstanding features other than a great deal of facial hair.

The man in the middle was anything but nondescript. He was a large man with a full head of black hair even though he appeared to be in his fifties. He was muscular with large hands that he kept clenching and unclenching. He didn't look happy to see them at all. His voice was a low bass rumble and he quickly took command. "Well, well, I see that you were able to get around our welcoming and figured out that I am the one you need to talk to. Did you bring it?"

Jack and David had stepped forward and Jack answered him. "Yes, I brought it. But that doesn't mean I am going to give it to you."

The large man smiled, "Oh, I believe that you will give it to me very soon."

David spoke up, "You are a hard person to find Amjad."

The large man turned his eyes to David and laughed. "Yes David Zahavy, you're right, I am hard to find. I'm even harder to beat once you find me."

Laura murmured from the back of the group. "Well, we know who has the corner on the pride market around here."

Amjad ignored her and her comment completely. Turning back to Jack he asked, "What price are you asking for the nail?"

"I want to know what your message about the ASF's secret leaders meant and where I can find them." Jack reached into his belt pack and produced the nail wrapped in a soft cloth.

Amjad's attention was fastened on the nail completely. "My message is that the real leaders of the Arab Strike Force are here in Basra and are presently concluding a deal with the government of Syria to pull a preemptive assault on Israel. I really expected you yesterday and it may already be too late to stop the signing of the agreement."

David stared at the Arab. "Why would Syria attack Israel? They know that they will lose more than the Golan Heights if they try that. Damascus will end up as a glowing crater in the desert."

Amjad laughed. "You of all people should know that nothing in the Middle East is straight-forward and simple. Listen! Iran has developed enough nuclear bombs and has them mounted on missiles aimed at every Israeli city. If they attempt to attack Syria with nuclear weapons that, will give Iran the reason they need to wipe Israel off the map! They also have added fifty thousand troops to the Syrian army which is massing on the border right now. They aren't going to be the losers in this war!"

David paled under the thought of unlimited nuclear exchanges between Israel and the two Arab countries. There wouldn't be any winners at all.

"Where is this meeting and how will stopping the meeting prevent the invasion?" Jack asked.

Amjad sat back in his seat. "The meeting is three buildings away to the east and the reason destroying the meeting will end the invasion plans, is because it will send a signal to Damascus and Tehran that Israel is aware of the plans and, because the leaders of the ASF have managed to get a copy of the Israeli battle plans for this scenario. That means they will have the once-in-a-lifetime chance to defeat the Israelis by beating them to every move. These plans are going to be exchanged for money and status in the soon-to-be all Arab Middle East. Now I have given you what you wanted. Give me the nail!

Jack said, "Just a minute, how do I know that what you told me is the truth? You could have lied and just made the whole thing up."

Amjad seemed to grow larger and darker as he rose from his seat. He became seemingly more powerful and dangerous. "I told you what you asked for. Give me the nail. NOW!!

Just then Gary Eisenthal stepped in front of Jack and whispered, "That isn't Amjad, that's Uthoth." He walked up to the table and stood before Amjad. "Uthoth" he said.

The large man smiled an evil smile. "Don't think that I am so easily impressed by you, little Garrison Eisenthal. I know you and how you chase around pestering my people with your little pleas for help. I'll crush you like a bug if you want to bother me. Just like this!"

The two Arabs who had been talking to Amjad suddenly started to shake and scream. Amjad's eyes never left those of Gary's. The man on Gary's left shrieked as his ribs snapped suddenly and his torso collapsed inward like it was being crushed by a giant fist. He fell quiet and just hung there, obviously dead but upright. The man on Gary's right fought the pressure on him until it became so great he was crushed and flung ten feet back into a wall and dropped to the floor like he was boneless. The man on the left also collapsed to the floor limply.

Jack tried to move and couldn't. He felt great pressure closing him in. He looked at Laura because he couldn't protect her and saw her standing there quietly with her eyes closed almost smiling. It hit him then what Gary had told him earlier about his powerlessness. As the pressure increased and he could actually hear his bones creaking, Jack started to pray and ask Yahshua to do the battle for him. As he felt the peace of the Lord settle on him the pressure dropped off and quickly disappeared. Jack then prayed for God to empower Gary Eisenthal in his battle with the demon.

Amjad/Uthoth suddenly reached out and hit Gary in the head with his fist. It was a mighty blow but all Gary did was stagger and continue to stare at the demon in front of him.

Jack looked around and saw that David, Mark, and Sarah were peaceful and that Sarah was quietly raising her hands in supplication to a loving God. Laura was still praying. He returned to praying that the demon facing Gary would be defeated in the name of Yahshua.

Pieces of furniture were being hurled through the air and directly at the people making up the team. But everything was being deflected before it hit any of the praying people or Gary.

Uthoth had grown in darkness and seemed to loom over Gary who had blood trickling out of the corner of his mouth from the blow.

Gary quietly said, "Uthoth! Look into my eyes and tell me what you see."

The demon caused Amjad to smile. "I'll see fear, that's what I'll see. He stared into Gary's eyes and suddenly blanched and backed up knocking over his chair. "I see the peace of Christ! Stay away from me!"

Gary quietly said, "Dear Lord Yahshua..."

Uthoth screamed, "Don't use that name in here!" He wheeled around and picked up a large sword that was standing against the wall behind him. He raised it to strike at Gary.

Gary didn't move and didn't defend himself. He merely said, "Lord Yahshua, I ask you to restrain this demon in your Name."

The sword fell out of Amjad/Uthoth hands and clattered to the floor. The large man seemed to be jerking and battling within himself. A fiendish scream or howl broke forth from his lips and he seemed to wither and shrink.

In a minute he stopped shaking and moving. When he looked up at Gary it wasn't as a demon but as a hunted enemy. Amjad reached behind his back and pulled out a large caliber handgun. Before he could aim it he was slapped off his feet in a spray of blood. The report of Craig's sniper rifle was muted by the sound suppressor and the tinkle of glass from the broken window. But it was enough to tell everyone where the shot had come from.

Gary said, "Thank you, Lord Yahshua..." and collapsed onto the floor.

Jack and David ran to his side. His breathing was normal but he had a real lump on his jaw from where he had been struck. "Jack said, "Let's get him outside."

They carried Gary outside and laid him on the grass. He moaned and kind of waved his hand to say that he was all right. David stood up and waved his arm at the darkness around them. In less than a minute the two soldiers were there. David asked Laura to stay with Gary while the rest of the team stopped the meeting before it was too late. He looked at them all. "I know what Tel Aviv's answer will be if Syria invades and Iraq threatens nuclear retaliation. If that happens you had bettered find something other than oil to run your cars on. There won't be any non-radioactive oil out of the middle east for something on the order of two thousand years!"

Grabbing their gear they headed for the third building to the east of them. Looking from behind a rock wall they saw several Syrian army guards and a personnel carrier parked in front of the building.

Mark looked at David. "You want this whole group eliminated?'

David nodded, "It's the only way we can prevent World War III. As soon as it goes nuclear the United States will be dragged into it and can China and/or Russia be far behind in an exchange like that? We are talking the end of the world!"

Mark said, "Okay then, here is what we'll do. We have enough RPGs to level the building and take out that PC in front. We need to get on the other side of this building so that we can cover the whole structure. Jack, you and Craig take half the RPGs and hightail it over there."

CHAPTER THIRTY-EIGHT

Inside the target building the meeting was drawing to a close and papers were being drawn up to be signed. Everyone was in a happy mood. This was something that should have been done long before this.

Outside, the team prepared to bring a little bit of hell on Earth to the participants of the meeting. David watched as Mark assigned the targets and the impact points to do the greatest damage. On both sides of the house they were using for cover, the rocket propelled grenades were inserted into the launchers and others prepared for quick reloading.

Mark set Craig to help Kevin with the other RPG while he made sure he and David could tag all three of the guards in front of the building. The first RPG Kevin fired would eliminate the personnel carrier and its machine gun.

Everything was ready and Mark looked at David for the go ahead. David nodded his head and Mark lined up the first guard in his telescopic sight. His finger took up the slack in the trigger and he was about to squeeze off the first shot as the signal to begin when he heard a small voice say "stop."

Mark shook his head and peered through the scope and again the voice, only louder this time…"Stop!" He looked around and saw Laura helping Gary limp up to their position. David turned around and glared at the slight man. "What's the matter? We don't have much time if we're going to stop this war!"

Gary was breathing hard and he put his hand up to have David wait a second while he got his breath back. He straightened up somewhat and asked David, "Don't shoot unless you're sure that it's the right thing to do."

David stared at him, "You know it's the right thing. These monsters will start a war that can't be won."

Gary was shaking his head, stronger now as he smiled at the Mossad man and asked, "Where did you get your information from?" Gary watched as understanding dawned on

David's face. "Right" Gary continued, "A demon lies more than it tells the truth. We can be sure of nothing if we don't find it out ourselves."

David frowned, "How are we going to find out what is going on here before it's over?"

About that time the doors to the building opened and a great number of people came out of the doorways and headed for vehicles drawing up to the front of the building. One man in uniform walked over near the team's location to smoke a cigarette. Sarah got up and walked out and spoke to him.

They talked for about three minutes and then the man followed Sarah back behind the wall. As they came around the wall Mark grabbed the man from behind in a choke hold and David pointed a pistol in his face. The man, a Syrian Army Major named Beheud, realized he was overmatched and quit struggling.

Jack and Craig rushed up at that time to see what had happened to the attack.

The Syrian Major's eyebrows went up another notch when he saw the heavily armed men.

David spoke fluid Arabic and asked the Major what the meeting was about. The Major refused to say anything.

For the first time in his life, David thought inside his head, "Dear God, what do I do now?" before he took any action. He clearly heard, *"Tell the truth."*

Blinking several times he shook his head. Then he looked at the Major and said, "We are a combined Israeli/American strike team. We've been given information that this meeting is between secret leaders of the ASF, Iran, and Syria to authorize an all-out assault on Israel by Syrian and Iranian forces. If that is the case then we will stop it now. If that is not the case you need to tell me what it is."

This really went against his training but David was learning to lean on God. All the other team members stood there gaping at David's admissions.

The Major thought for a second and said, "It is strange, but I believe you. The secret meeting here tonight was to sign a mutual defense pact between Syria and the Iranian Insurgency. We feel with our help they will be able to get rid of the madmen that are running their country. I don't know what devil gave you that strange information but for Allah's sake, don't destroy these people! They are not planning any harm to Israeli!"

David stood there undecided. Was Major Beheud telling the truth or lying?

Since he was cooperating, Mark loosened his hold on the Major.

The Major looked at David. "I wonder if you realize what would happen if you did destroy this meeting and the people here? I see you are using Soviet weapons but if any of you were caught then it would come out that Israel is supporting the government of Iran against its own people. Not to mention the military and political fallout such an act would have against your country."

He was about to continue when a voice called out for him. He held up his hands and said, "Let me handle this or there will be a battle." David watched him as he approached the corner of the wall. He called out to the person seeking him. "Hey! I'm over here taking a break. I'll be back in five minutes."

The other person was suspicious. "What are you taking a break over there for?"

The major looked at Sarah and wiggled his fingers at her. She walked over and looked around the corner at the other man.

Seeing the woman he laughed. "Major Beheud! I see your reputation is well deserved. Five minutes is all, huh? Okay, I'll cover for you, but hurry, one of the Iranian rebels is asking for you." He turned and walked back toward the building.

The Major and Sarah walked back to David. David held out his hand and shook the Major's. "Sorry about the misunderstanding. You were right when you wondered what devil gave us the information."

About that time Gary stepped into the conversation. "Yes, a devil named Amjad."

The Major shook his head. "I'll kill that snake next time I see him."

David smiled, "Well, then we've done you a service. He's already dead. Check his house. By the way, he killed the other two men you'll find there, actually squeezed them to death."

The Major frowned, "I think the world is a better place without him. But what I cannot figure out is how you managed to get here without any of our troops knowing about it."

David clasped him on the shoulder and walked him to the end of the wall. "Let's just say that we are on the same side this time and a terrible mistake was prevented. About how we got here, well, we have to have some secrets you know?"

The Major stopped and looked at the shadowy figures facing him in the gloom. He saluted and said, "I'm glad to meet you. You have changed my impression of many things tonight. Don't worry about my raising any alarm. It would be egg on my face since I'm in charge of the defense of this area. Goodbye." He turned and casually walked back to the meeting.

The team policed up the area and extracted out of town and back to the Sand Snake as quickly as possible. Three hours later they were back in Tel Aviv.

CHAPTER THIRTY-NINE

As the Boeing 747 winged its way across the Atlantic, Laura was fast asleep in her first class seat. Jack looked out the window at the water seven miles below the aircraft and tried to bring their latest adventure to some sort of closure.

The Mossad had cracked down on the cohorts of the ASF in Israel and either killed them, arrested them, or had driven them out of the nation altogether. Since all the members of the ASF that the Israelis knew about were in jail in America, there had been no more attacks or incidences of violence from that group since the program had begun.

David had been offered yet another promotion to management and had again politely refused it. This resulted in his being 'promoted' to strategy manager for agents on the street. He liked it because he could now get involved in everything the Mossad was doing if he wanted to. Also, he was tasked with field training for all senior agents. If the Mossad was upset about his conversion to Christianity, they didn't show it. They gave him great praise for his involvement in the entire ASF plot resolution.

Sarah had resigned from the Mossad with David's blessings to take the number two position at Mark's Counter Terrorism and Security Company. It was obvious to the most casual observer that she was a natural for the position since she was wearing a beautiful engagement ring. She said that Mark was going to make an 'honest' woman out of her. He just smiled and agreed. The only question was, 'who would really be in charge?'

Mark actually had a breather from government assignments and was reviewing the different possibilities being offered for his services. Cutting it down to one, as the most interesting and lucrative, he had asked Sarah if she would like to have their honeymoon in scenic, picturesque rural Russia.

She reportedly had smiled and asked what caliber weapons he wanted her to pack for the trip. Jack could see that they would make a great couple since they had so many things in common.

Mark reported one other thing that was very interesting. It seems that they were joined in Tel Aviv by Jim Ballard, the Christian Prophet and Evangelist that had prayed to baptize Jack and Laura in the Holy Spirit. It seemed that God had sent him to Israel to find Mark and Sarah and to pray and baptize them, also. Mark admitted that it was the first time he fell on the floor because of God.

Christi and her band had already left for the states and the boys were headed back to their military units.

The eOne Software Company had been exonerated by the Mossad and Israeli government of having any involvement in the poisoning affair and had returned to designing and making software with the public's approval.

Most Jews in Tel Aviv had managed to justify God's rescue as a definite sign that Yahshua wasn't needed even though it was obviously through the Son of God they had been saved. Go figure. Life returned to normal for most residents.

The ASF terrorists directly involved in the poisoning plot were scheduled to go to trial in about a month. The remainder of the group was being held in a military prison somewhere in the Southwestern United States while the courts fought over the concept of 'corporate guilt'. Privately, many people thought the ASF activists would die of old age before they had their day in court.

Jack thought about returning to his own company and running it again. Somehow that had lost a lot of its original charm for him. He was smart enough to realize that he had been moved into a highly-charged wider world over the last three months. He also realized that God was using these "incidents" to train him for service. By implication, that meant that there was something else to come their way.

But he didn't allow the worry that used to plague him about things like this, to bother him. He just gave it up to Yahshua and waited on the Lord.

This was where the Lord wanted him to be. Ready, trained, and in submission to God's will.

The Crossfire team returns in **"*Believer's Crossfire.*"**

If this story has awakened your spirit or moved you to seek the love of Christ and His power for your life, whether you've never accepted Jesus as your savior or you've fallen away, repeat the following prayer and begin a most wonderful journey into eternal life with Him today.

Father God in heaven, As You said in Your Holy Word, (Romans 10:9) that if we confess the Lord our God and believe in our hearts that God raised Jesus from the dead, we shall be saved.

(The prayer on the next page is a sample prayer when asking Jesus into your heart as your Savior. You can also pray this in your own words.)

Salvation Prayer

Dear God in heaven, I come to you in the name of Jesus. I confess to You that I am a sinner, and I am sorry for my sins and the life that I have lived; I need your forgiveness. I believe that your only begotten Son Jesus Christ shed His precious blood on the cross at Calvary and died for my sins, and I am now willing to turn from my sin.

Right now I confess Jesus as the Lord of my life and my soul. With all my heart, I truly believe that your Holy Spirit raised Jesus from the dead. Today I accept Jesus Christ as my personal Savior and according to Your Word, right now I am saved.

I thank you Jesus, for your unlimited grace which has saved me from my sins. I thank you Jesus that your grace that never leads to license, but rather it always leads to repentance. Therefore Lord Jesus, transform my life so that I may bring glory and honor to you alone and not to myself.

I Thank you Lord Jesus, for dying for me at Calvary and giving me eternal life.

Amen.

If you just said this prayer and you meant it with all your heart, believe that you are now saved and have been born again.

You may ask, "Now that I am saved, what do I do next?" First of all you need to get into a spirit-filled, bible-based church that teaches the Scriptures, and you need to study God's Word.

Once you have found a church home, you will want to become water-baptized. By accepting Christ you are baptized in the spirit, but it is through water-baptism that you publically announce your obedience to the Lord Jesus. Water baptism is a symbol of your salvation from the dead. You were dead but now you live, for Jesus Christ has redeemed you for a price! The price was His atoning death on the cross. May God Bless You!

www.ingramcontent.com/pod-product-compliance
Lightning Source LLC
Chambersburg PA
CBHW071329250626
47159CB00004B/1526